The Great Summer Camp Catastrophe

THE Great Summer Camp Catastrophe

Jean Van Leeuwen
pictures by Diane deGroat

Dial Books for Young Readers
New York

Published by Dial Books for Young Readers
A Division of Penguin Books USA Inc.
375 Hudson Street
New York, New York 10014
Text copyright © 1992 by Jean Van Leeuwen
Pictures copyright © 1992 by Diane deGroat
All rights reserved
Printed in the U.S.A.
First Edition
3 5 7 9 10 8 6 4 2

Library of Congress Cataloging in Publication Data
Van Leeuwen, Jean.
The great summer camp catastrophe
Jean Van Leeuwen.—1st ed.
p.   cm.
Summary: Three mice who live in a department store are
dismayed when they are accidentally shipped in a care package
to a ten-year-old boy in a summer camp in Vermont, but after
joining in a few of the activities they find that they like camp life.
ISBN 0-8037-1106-9 (trade)—ISBN 0-8037-1107-7 (lib.)
[1. Mice—Fiction. 2. Camps—Fiction.] I. Title.
PZ7.V3273Gu 1992 91-18487 [Fic]—dc20 CIP AC

*For Sam Gavril,
Marvin's longtime fan,
with love*

Contents

The Great
Summer Camp
Catastrophe

1

I Have
a Rude Awakening

"Wake up, Marvin!"

A voice is whispering in my ear. I attempt to open one eye, but sleep has me wrapped in a dense gray fog.

"Marvin!"

The voice is insistent. I recognize it as Fats's. What could he want that is important? "Go away," I mumble, burying my head in the pillow.

"But you've got to see this. It's a miracle!"

Now he is jumping up and down on my stomach.

Oof! I am a tough guy, but this is a heavyweight mouse. Reluctantly I open my eyes. And there is Fats's face, grinning from ear to ear, an inch from my own.

"Just come and look, Marvin." He drags me, blinking, from my cozy canopy bed to the window. Pulling back the ruffled curtain, he points.

"There," he says.

All I see are ice cream cones. Single dips and double dips. Strawberry, peach, lemon, and lime. I must be dreaming. But this dream could belong only to Fats, the world's biggest food maniac. How did I get into Fats's dream?

I rub my eyes. I know I'm awake. And I know where I am: in the dollhouse on the top shelf in the toy department of Macy's in New York City, where I live with my gang. I look again.

The ice cream cones are still there.

"Isn't it amazing?" murmurs Fats. He has a silly grin on his face, and his ample stomach is actually quivering. Fats always acts ridiculous around food.

"It certainly is," agrees a voice behind us. Raymond, the other member of my gang, peers through his spectacles out the window. "Those ice cream cones look almost real."

"Almost?" Fats looks suddenly stricken. "You mean they *aren't* real?"

"Of course not," says Raymond in his calm school-teacherish voice. "Would real ice cream cones hang from the ceiling? Would real ice cream cones just sit there, not melting? These are cardboard. I saw the decorators hanging them when I got up this morning."

I look once more. Sure enough, all the ice cream cones have strings attached.

"Cardboard," I pronounce. "Obviously. I knew it all the time."

Fats still can't believe it. "Maybe *some* of them are real," he says hopefully. "We could just touch a few and see."

I glance at the clock above the games and puzzles counter. There is nearly an hour before the store opens, plenty of time for a look around. Fats could be right. The decorations might include free samples. Anyway, I always like to know what is going on in the toy department.

"Okay, gang," I tell them. "We're going to check out the ice cream cones."

Cautiously I poke my nose outside our front door. I look to the left. I look to the right. I see no decorators, salesclerks, or managers.

"The coast is clear," I announce.

We step outside. From our perch high above the doll counter, we have a perfect view of the toy department. The first thing I notice is a bright green

5

banner strung between the games counter and the music counter.

"Does it say 'Free Ice Cream'?" asks Fats, still hopeful.

He looks at Raymond. Raymond is an educated mouse. He taught himself to read back in the days when we lived in a movie theater, from the newspapers people left under their seats. When we moved to Macy's, he discovered the book department and moved on to heavier stuff: dictionaries, atlases, the history of the world. His greatest achievement was reading the entire set of Encyclopedia Britannica, Volume I to XVI.

"Summertime . . . And the Living is Easy," reads Raymond.

"Ah," sighs Fats. Easy is the way he likes to live.

Now I notice that these decorators have used more than ice cream cones to show the easy life. Floating near the ceiling are balloons in the same colors of pink, orange, green, and yellow. And on top of the counters are displays of beach umbrellas, beach towels, beach balls, boats, floats, all kinds of beach toys.

I look at my gang. My gang looks at me. I can see we all have the same thought. It is why we've lived all these months in Macy's toy department.

"Come on," I say. "Let's try out the new toys."

Dangling in front of my nose is a curly ribbon attached to a pink balloon. I grab it. "Watch this," I say, wrapping the ribbon around my waist.

Boldly I jump into space.

"Marvin, what are you doing?" cries Raymond. He is a worrier as well as a thinker.

But I am floating gently downward, past the shelves of doll furniture, baby dolls, dolls from other countries. This is how it must feel to parachute from an airplane, like the soldiers in all those war movies we used to watch in our days at the movie theater. It's like flying, but with time to look around.

I drift past the doll carriages. Too soon my feet touch the floor. I unwrap the ribbon and let my parachute float back to the ceiling.

"It's great!" I call to my gang. "You've got to try it!"

Raymond and Fats look doubtful. They've never had my daring. But finally Raymond wraps himself up like a package and takes the leap. And then Fats. On his way down he can't resist taking a bite out of a passing ice cream cone. He lands in a heap at my feet, spitting out something soggy and disgusting.

"Just cardboard," he mutters sadly.

He goes off to look for the real thing, while Raymond and I check out the latest summer toys. Our first stop is a mountain of beach balls.

"I am the strongest mouse in the world," I declare. "Look at this." And I lift a striped beach ball twenty times my size over my head.

"That's nothing," replies Raymond. "Look at this." He lifts a polka-dot ball with one hand.

"Oh, yeah?" I retort. "That's child's play. Look at this." I balance a Mickey Mouse ball on one finger.

Raymond can't top that one. We move on to a display of toy sailboats. There are chubby old-fashioned boats and sporty racers and a strange-looking model with twin bottoms. Raymond climbs on board the biggest of them all, long and shiny and bright blue, with about four sails. He stands on its front deck, staring dreamily into the distance.

"What are you doing?" I demand.

"Pretending," Raymond says softly. "I've always wanted to go to sea."

I never knew this about Raymond. Sailing seems kind of quiet to me. Personally, I prefer faster, more adventurous modes of transportation.

Just as I have this thought, my eye falls on something I hadn't noticed before. Sitting on the table where my favorite electric train used to be is a plastic wading pool filled with water. And bobbing on the water is a whole fleet of motorboats.

Now this is more my speed. In an instant I am up over the side of the wading pool. Picking the flashiest red motorboat, I jump into the driver's seat. I flip the *On* switch, and its engine roars to life.

I am off on a wild splashing ride. I dodge other boats. I crisscross over giant waves. Around and around I go, faster and faster. Spray is in my eyes and my fur is soaking wet, but I am shouting with joy. This is the life I was meant to lead.

My noise brings Raymond and Fats to investigate. And soon the three of us are racing one another: my incredible red machine against Raymond's long black cruiser and Fats's peppy little blue boat. Naturally I am in the lead, when suddenly I feel my engine hesitate.

"Faster!" I shout, looking over my shoulder. Fats is gaining on me.

But instead my boat goes slower. And then, incredibly, it stops. There I am, dead in the water in the middle of the wading pool.

"I win!" cries Fats, zipping by me.

Raymond goes by too, then circles back. "What happened?" he asks.

"I don't know," I snap grumpily. I hate to lose.

Among Raymond's other talents, he is a skilled mechanic. He learned from copies of *Popular Mechanics* he scavenged under the movie theater seats. One look at my engine tells him all he needs to know. "Your battery is dead," he announces.

Fats has been circling around me, cackling, "I won! I won!" But now his boat seems to have lost its pep.

"Hey, what's going on?" he asks, as it too comes to a stop.

"These boats are run by batteries," Raymond explains. "Batteries run for only so long and then they have to be recharged."

Fats and I climb aboard his boat. Raymond docks it at the side of the pool, and once again we are back on dry, boring land.

"I think my battery needs to be recharged too," says Fats.

I look at him, puzzled. Fats is not a motorboat.

"I'm hungry," he moans softly. "All those ice cream cones were cardboard, and I couldn't find any that were real, and I *need* ice cream. Strawberry or black raspberry. Those are my favorite flavors, but I'll take anything. It doesn't even have to be ice cream. A pickle would do. Or maybe a chocolate chip cookie. Actually, a chocolate chip cookie would be fine."

Food, food. It's all Fats ever thinks about. Still, I have to admit all that beach ball lifting and motorboat racing has given me an appetite. And there is still a half hour before the store opens.

I give in. "Okay, okay. Time for a food raid."

With the ease of long practice, we slip out of the toy department. Keeping a sharp eye out for salesclerks, we make our way past piles of luggage, past the TV sets where we have whiled away many a night watching old gangster movies. Straight ahead is the escalator. We jump on, take a fast ride up, and find ourselves in Fats's favorite of all favorite places, his idea of heaven: Macy's delicatessen.

Actually, it is more than a delicatessen. The delis I knew when I lived on the streets were quite appetizing, with their salami and pastrami, their pumpernickel and rye, their Swiss cheese and potato salad and juicy dill pickles. But this one is even more delicious. Besides basic Swiss, it has all kinds of exotic cheeses, from buffalo mozzarella to double Gloucester to Muenster with caraway seeds. There are jams and jellies, honeys and mustards, jars of oil with strange branches inside. Then there are the fancy foods with fancy names: artichokes, anchovies, oysters, jalapeño peppers, and—my own personal favorite—caviar. There are crackers in tins, nuts in jars, popcorn in pails. And recently a new counter has been added, selling homemade cookies for those with a sweet tooth like Fats. The delicatessen even has a fancy new name: "The Educated Palate."

Fats doesn't waste time. He heads straight for the chocolate chip cookies. Raymond samples the latest flavors in cheeses, while I climb up to check on the caviar supply.

Caviar. It is so special that the clerks keep it apart from everything else, high on a shelf above the cheeses. I press my nose against a glass jar, gazing at the inky black bubbles, my mouth watering as I remember their sweet-salty taste. Counting the jars, I see there are only five left. If I took one, would anyone notice?

As I hesitate, trying to decide, I hear voices. Salesclerks, I know instantly. Female. Two of them. From my high perch, I spot them riding up the escalator. Now they are getting off. They are heading this way.

In a split second I am off the shelf. "Raymond!" I hiss. He abandons a hunk of Stilton and follows me. We sprint for the cookie counter. "Fats!"

Where is he? I look in the glass case. All the chocolate chip cookies are gone, and so is Fats. Did he move on to demolish the oatmeal cookies? Or polish off a bag of jelly beans?

The voices come closer.

"Fats!"

No answer. He could have wandered off to find a pickle.

Then I hear a tiny familiar sound. Crunch, sigh. It seems to come from a pile of cardboard boxes behind the cookie counter.

"Fats, where are you?"

"Here," comes the faint reply.

I follow the crunches to the top of the pile. I jump

inside a box. Raymond follows, pulling the lid down just as the voices arrive at the cookie counter.

"And how is your arthritis, Maggie?"

"Not so good, Selma. It's all this rain we've been having."

It is dark inside this box. But I know it is the right one. I am surrounded by the smell of chocolate. And that sound: crunch, sigh, crunch, sigh.

"Ssssh!" I whisper. "Salesclerks."

At last Fats is silent. I strain my ears to make out what is going on. Have the clerks moved on, or are they still at the cookie counter? Has the store opened? Is there still time to make a getaway?

I nudge Raymond. "Boost me up," I order.

Standing on his shoulders, I can just reach the slit at the top of the box. Cautiously I peek out.

And then several things happen all at once.

The box is suddenly lifted. I am thrown from my perch, crashing down on top of Raymond. And then it drops with a thud. Ouch! I bounce off something hard and am buried under a pile of something else, something round like marbles, but light and dry. I try to dig out, only I keep falling back. I'm drowning in these strange marbles.

At last I grasp something firm. I am climbing, up, up toward that slit of light. I'm almost there when I hear the sound of ripping tape. And the top of the box is closed, the slit of light gone.

That is when I hear the voices again.

"Well, Selma. All finished?"

"That's it, Maggie. The last gift box, ready to be shipped."

2

I Go on a Terrifying Journey

Ready to be shipped! I can't believe my ears. And then it dawns on me what has happened. We have wandered unsuspectingly into a gift box and are about to be mailed—across town, out of town, maybe even out of the country. This is my worst nightmare come true. And all because of Fats and his big appetite.

We've got to get out of this box. And fast. Immediately my razor-sharp brain has the answer. We'll chew our way out. In the past we have chewed through grocery bags, shopping bags, and knitting bags. Once Fats even ate his way under a wooden door. A cardboard box can't be that hard. But we have to move fast.

I rally my gang like a good leader should. "Raymond, Fats! Over here!"

"Over where?" whimpers Fats. "I can't see anything."

"In the corner," I say. "Where we're going to chew our way to freedom."

In a moment they are standing beside me. "Okay," I tell them. "Start chewing."

"But my mouth is tired," complains Fats. "I just finished a whole bag of chocolate chip cookies."

"Do you want to be shipped somewhere far far away?" I ask him. "Somewhere where there are no chocolate chip cookies?"

"Okay, okay," he mumbles. "I'll chew."

I shove aside those annoying marbles. Now I realize what they are: the little white Styrofoam things that salesclerks dump into boxes when they pack them. They're to make sure we don't get broken. I take a big bite of box. But just as I do, it is lifted once again. Lifted and thrown down. We are thrown down too in a tangle of teeth and legs and tails.

Then, plunk. Something is piled on top of our box. Plunk, plunk, plunk. More heavy objects are dropped on us.

"The boxes are being stacked," Raymond whispers in my ear.

With each plunk, our box shivers and we quiver. And then the whole stack is in motion. Squeak, creak. Squeak, creak.

"What's that?" moans Fats.

"We're on a cart," Raymond replies. "On our way to the shipping room."

The cart careens around corners and bounces over bumps. Squeak, creak, squeak! Whoever is pushing it is a crazy driver. Then suddenly there is a loud clang, bang! And the bottom falls out of the floor.

"It's the end of the world!" squeals Fats.

"It's only the elevator," Raymond reassures him.

Down, down, down we plummet. I feel as if the bottom has fallen out of my stomach, and my left ear hurts. Next to me, Fats is gnawing nervously on something. I realize it is my left ear.

"Stop chewing," I growl.

"Sorry," he mumbles.

At last the elevator shudders to a stop. Clang, bang! The door opens, and once more the cart lurches forward.

"Ah," sighs Fats in relief.

But there is even worse to come. For we have reached the dreaded shipping room. Even sealed inside our box, we can still make out all the noise: machinery clanking, boxes thumping, people shouting, truck doors slamming, and engines starting up, getting ready to carry gift boxes to faraway places.

It occurs to me that our situation is desperate. It is now or never. Live or die. Chew or be shipped.

Tough guy that I am, I rise to the occasion.

"Chew, gang!" I implore them. "Chew as you have never chewed before."

Hardly are the words out of my mouth before our box is flying through the air. The next few minutes are a confusion of being tossed, turned, stamped, piled up, and thrown onto some kind of moving machine, like an escalator but noisier. ("Must be a conveyor belt," decides Raymond, always thinking.) And then we are thrown one more time.

It is this last one that does it. Already we are bruised and battered. This time I bump heads with Fats and tangle tails with Raymond. And then I crash into something even harder than Fats's head.

I stagger. I sway. I see stars. Vaguely I am aware of a door slamming, an engine roaring to life.

And then I am out like a light.

When I wake up, I have no idea where I am. It is never this dark in my dollhouse. Why am I lying on a bed of marbles? Why is it moving? And then everything comes back to me. I am not in my dollhouse. I am not even in Macy's. I am sealed inside a box sealed inside a truck on its way to an unknown destination. We have been shipped.

Sitting up, I notice that my head aches and my tail aches and there is a queasy feeling in the pit of my stomach. I tend to get carsick on long journeys. For a moment I am filled with despair.

But only for a moment. Then I remember who I am: Merciless Marvin the Magnificent, tough leader of a tough gang. I have been in difficult spots before. And each time I have led my gang to victory. There was the time when, inspired by all the gangster movies we'd seen in the movie theater, we engineered the robbery of a cheese shop. I saved us from being sent up the river to prison. And the time we came up against the wily criminal who had kidnapped Macy's Santa Claus. I traveled all the way to Brooklyn to bring him back in time for Christmas. Not to mention the time Fats disappeared without a trace. I faced vicious doormen and Fifth Avenue nannies and the wilderness of Central Park and still came out on top. I know I can do it again.

I get to my feet, shaking off my insignificant aches and pains.

"Gang," I say, "I'm going to get us out of this."

There is no answer.

"Gang?"

Where can they be? Now that I am used to the dark, I begin to make out my surroundings. Next to me is a glass jar filled with peanuts. This must be what knocked me unconscious. Near it is a tin of popcorn. And a bag of pretzels. Now I see why Fats chose this box. It is filled with things he loves to eat.

Then, unbelievably, I hear it. Crunch, sigh.

Following the sound, I discover Fats. He is inside a bag of jelly beans, lying on a bed of jelly beans, his mouth stuffed full of jelly beans.

"What are you doing?" I demand.

"I've never had the gourmet flavors before," he replies. "Have you tried watermelon? Or passion fruit? Or tangerine?" He thrusts a jelly bean at me.

I push it away. "How can you eat at a time like this?"

"Well," says Fats a little sheepishly. "You were asleep and Raymond was asleep. I was just keeping my strength up."

"Raymond asleep?" I can't believe it. Without me to lead them, my gang totally falls apart.

Fats points to the popcorn tin, from under which protrudes a familiar-looking tail. I give it a pull.

"Help!" calls a familiar-sounding voice.

Raymond is not asleep. He is trapped under five pounds of popcorn.

Using all my muscles, I manage to tip the tin, and Raymond crawls out. "Thanks, Marvin," he says.

He retrieves his spectacles, and I retrieve Fats from the jelly bean bag. Finally I have both their attention.

"Gang," I begin. "Our situation is desperate. We are trapped in a gift box packed in a truck rolling down a highway. Each minute takes us farther from Macy's. Who knows what dangers await us? Who knows if we will ever see our dollhouse home again? It does not look good for the good guys. But—" I launch into my most rousing pep talk—"we must not give up. We are tough! We are smart! We are brave! Remember your names."

They look puzzled. It was a long time ago, those days in the Bijou Theater, when I trained Raymond and Fats to be in my gang.

Then the light dawns. "Raymond the Rat," murmurs Raymond.

"Exactly," I confirm. I gave him his name to make him think tough.

"Fats the Fuse!" cries Fats.

"Precisely," I agree. Fats's name was in honor of

his love for explosives. His favorite part of gangster movies was always when the safe was blown up. "And I am Merciless Marvin the Magnificent, in case you've forgotten. There is only one way out of this tight spot."

"I know!" says Fats eagerly. "We'll blast!"

"Don't be ridiculous." I glare at him.

"We'll chew," suggests Raymond quietly.

"Absolutely," I reply. "And I don't mean jelly beans."

We attack the corner of that box with the energy of desperation. Chomp, chomp, chomp. Three sets of teeth with a single mission. We slice swiftly through the cardboard. It won't be long until we breathe the air of freedom once again.

Chomp, chomp, chomp. I notice that my teeth are no longer slicing so swiftly. They have come up against something hard, something with a sticky, gluey taste.

"Tape," I say disgustedly. "Wouldn't you know it?"

"Yuck!" exclaims Fats. "Tape has such a bad flavor. Like old sneakers."

"Never mind," I tell him. "Just keep going. Bite and chew! Bite and chew!"

The road beneath us has grown bumpy. The box bounces up and down. I bite my tongue, but I keep on chewing.

Chomp, chomp, chomp.

"We're nearly there. A few more bites, and we're home free."

Chomp, chomp, chomp.

"Mmmphf!" Raymond seems to be trying to say something.

"Don't talk. Chew!"

"Bud Marbfin," he sputters. "We shtopped."

I pause in mid-bite. It's true. No longer do I hear the hum of the highway. No longer do I feel the floor beneath us shaking. What has happened? Has the driver stopped for a cup of coffee? Or can it be that we have reached our destination?

A door slams. Another one, much closer, opens.

I have barely time to shout, "Hold on to your hats, gang!" before it is happening all over again.

Tumbling and turning, bouncing and jouncing, upside down and inside out, and then—finally—stillness. I lie there, dazed, with one thought spinning through my head: we have been delivered.

Then, above us, I hear a new sound. *Ripppp!*

The box is being opened.

"Hide!" I hiss, and we dive under those marbles, all the way down to the bottom of the box.

Hands reach in, pushing aside the marbles, taking things out. Voices exclaim, "Oh, boy, peanuts!"

"Popcorn, my favorite!" "Hey, pass me the jelly beans."

Boys, I observe, using my well-developed detective skills. Two of them. About ten years old.

"Those are *my* jelly beans!" squeaks Fats, and I clap a paw over his mouth.

The hands search for more goodies. I press flat against the side of the box, my heart beating in my ears like a drum. This is it. We are about to be discovered.

But instead of discovering me, the hands find the chocolate chip cookie bag. "That's weird," says a voice. "There's a cookie bag, but no cookies."

"Rats!" says the other voice.

At the mention of his name, Raymond trembles beside me.

Then, amazingly, things get calm. The lid of the box closes. The box moves one more time, but slowly, as if it is being nudged across the floor. There is a squeaking sound above us, like bedsprings.

We are safe, I think, at least for the moment. An empty box shoved under a bed.

"So you think your mom will send you great stuff like this every week?"

"She promised to send me a care package every week I'm at camp."

"Wow! That's eight great care packages!"

"Camp?" I whisper. "Did he say camp?"

"What's a care package?" asks Fats.

"It's when you send stuff to someone to show you care," Raymond explains.

Camp, boys, care packages. My brain is working overtime, trying to make sense of all this. Can it be that we have been gift wrapped, shipped, and delivered to a ten-year-old boy at camp?

"Raymond," I whisper again. "Isn't camp in the country?"

"Right," confirms Raymond.

My heart sinks.

"Gang," I say. "We've got to get out of here."

3

I Make the Acquaintance
of the Country

I sleep an uneasy sleep, full of dreams. All of them
are bad.

In one, I am climbing a mountain. This is no ordinary mountain. It is made of candy wrappers. But
every time I almost make it to the top, I start sliding
down. I'm buried in candy wrappers: Snickers, Nes-
tlé Crunch, Peter Paul Almond Joy. I realize that I
will never get to the top. There are millions of them.
These are the wrappers of every candy bar Fats has
ever eaten.

In another, I am a prisoner of war. I am locked in
a torture chamber. Bare light bulbs shine in my eyes,
like in all the prisoner of war movies. The enemy

general is interrogating me, but I refuse to answer. I will not betray my country. "We'll see about that," snarls the general. I look him fearlessly in the eye. It is then I notice that the general is a ten-year-old boy. Another boy steps forward, carrying a bowl. "Perhaps this will refresh your memory," says the general. A spoon comes toward me, piled high with those little white marbles we were packed in.

"Not those!" I gasp. I will never betray my country. But I can't eat those marbles.

Suddenly I hear the sound of trumpets. It's the cavalry come to rescue me, just like in the Western movies. "Here I am!" I cry. These trumpets are hurting my ears. Why don't they stop playing and get me out of jail?

"Stop the music!" I shout, and I wake up.

I am not a prisoner of war, I see, only a prisoner of a care package. But I can still hear those awful trumpets.

"It must be reveille," whispers Raymond.

"Ravioli? Did someone say ravioli?" Instantly Fats is awake and drooling.

"Not ravioli," corrects Raymond. "Reveille."

"What's that?" I demand.

"It's the way they wake you up," explains Raymond. "In the army or at camp."

This reveille must have been invented by an enemy general to torture prisoners of war.

The campers seem to agree. I hear one of the voices from last night complaining sleepily, "Get up? It's the middle of the night."

"It's cold!" moans another.

"I think I'll skip breakfast," mumbles a third.

But then a deeper voice says, "No one skips breakfast in this cabin!"

It's the general, I think.

"It's the counselor," says Raymond.

Suddenly bedsprings squeak, feet hit the floor. Voices, still complaining, ask, "How come it's freezing in July?"

"Anyone seen my Yankees sweatshirt?"

"Hey, watch who you're stepping on."

There must be seven or eight boys in this cabin, I calculate. They are falling all over one another, looking for their clothes. Hands fumble close to our box, zippers zip, shoes drop.

"Everyone ready?" asks the deep voice. "Let's go."

"I can't find my other sneaker," protests someone.

Doors bang, feet pound across the floor.

"Beat you to the lodge!"

"No way!"

"Hey, you guys, wait for me!"

And then, abruptly, everything is quiet.

Inside our box we huddle together, listening. All I can hear is the soft ticktock, ticktock of a clock somewhere in the room. A minute goes by. Another minute. Nothing happens.

"I think they're gone," I whisper.

"To breakfast," adds Raymond.

"Ravioli for breakfast," sighs Fats. "What a good idea!" As usual, he is a little confused.

Breakfast should take at least a half hour, maybe more if these campers are hearty eaters. Now is our chance for some fresh air and a look at this place we've been shipped to.

"Gang," I say, "it's time to get out of this box."

We dig our way out from under all those marbles. Standing on Raymond's shoulders, I lift the lid of the box.

Fresh air at last! After spending hours and hours trapped in a gift box, all I want to do is breathe in and out. Real air. It smells delicious.

"What do you see?" asks Raymond.

"Not much," I report. Just as I deduced, we have been stored under a bed. In the dim light I can make out other objects near us: a crumpled towel, a couple of inside-out socks, a leaning stack of magazines, a rubber boot, a baseball mitt, a baseball cap, some wadded-up candy wrappers. But that's all I can see.

"Come on, gang," I order.

With a few tugs, Raymond and Fats emerge. We walk around, stretching our legs, brushing away the leftover marbles that cling to our fur. I check once more to make sure the coast is clear. Then I step out from under the bed.

Beds. This is the first thing I see. Beds and more beds. They fill the room. They are even stacked on top of one another. Bunk beds, these are called. I know them from Macy's furniture department, where we liked to do a little bed-bouncing now and then.

". . . seven, eight, nine," counts Raymond. "There must be eight boys and a counselor in this cabin."

A cabin is what it is. Everything is made of logs, even the bunk beds. And everything looks about a hundred years old. There are windows, but no glass in them, only caved-in screens. Spiderwebs fill the corners. Dust balls roll across the floor. The last time I left Macy's, I lived a life of luxury in an apartment on Fifth Avenue. This place is a long way from Fifth Avenue.

"Marvin," calls Raymond. "Look at this."

He has wandered into the next room. It is a living room, with a stone fireplace, a couple of broken-down couches, lamps with crooked shades, a rickety table, and something on the wall that looks like tree branches but, I realize, is a set of deer antlers. Raymond is not looking at these. He is gazing at something above the fireplace. "I believe I have found a clue," he announces.

Instantly my great detective brain clicks into high gear. I look where he is looking. But all I see is a framed picture of a lopsided green blob. It doesn't look like anything. It must be modern art.

"Uh—right," I say. "Some clue."

Raymond jumps up on the mantle to take a closer look. He twirls his whiskers, as he always does when he is thinking. "Very interesting."

"Fascinating," I agree. I can't stand it anymore. "What is so interesting?" I demand.

"This map of Vermont," replies Raymond.

So that is what the green blob is. Raymond should know. He has read the Rand McNally World Atlas from cover to cover. He knows the location of countries I never even knew existed.

"The interesting thing," Raymond continues, "is this red X in the upper left-hand corner. It says 'Camp Moose-a-honk.' This must be the name of the camp. If I am correct, we know our location. We are somewhere at the top of Vermont."

The top of Vermont. It looks far away. It sounds

far away. "Is the top of Vermont far from New York City?" I ask.

"I'm afraid so," says Raymond.

As I am digesting this discouraging information, I notice Fats. He has been sniffing in corners, looking for lost candy bars. Now he stops at a screen door. He takes a deep breath. He starts to twitch. And suddenly he is bouncing up and down. "I smell it!" he cries.

If it's Fats, it has to be food.

"Ravioli?" I ask.

"No," he says softly. "A Christmas tree!"

One of the high points of Fats's life, ranking just below his discovery of Wisconsin cheddar cheese and his invention of the peanut butter, watermelon pickle, and tortilla chip sandwich, was the time we decorated our own little Christmas tree at Macy's. I remember how it smelled, like the polish the cleaning people use on the wood cabinets in the toy department. I inhale, and I can smell it too.

"Oh, there's another one!" squeals Fats. "And another one. Come quick, Marvin!"

Raymond and I hurry to the door. As far as my eye can see, there are nothing but Christmas trees.

"But why are there so many?" Fats sounds bewildered. "It isn't even winter."

"These are not Christmas trees," Raymond replies calmly. "They are pine trees. They grow here. This is the country, you know."

The country. I have never been to the country before, unless you count Central Park. I step through a slit in the screen door, and suddenly I am in a new world. This world is green. There are green Christmas trees and green bushes and green grass beneath our feet. And it is wide—much wider than Central Park. There you know there are buildings just beyond the trees. But here the trees and mountains and sky seem to go on forever. And then there is the smell. It smells like the city does sometimes just after a rain shower: all scrubbed down and brand-new. Mixed in with that spicy Christmas tree smell are grassy, flowery aromas, so sweet that they tickle my nose. One more thing I notice about the country: it is quiet. My ears are accustomed to the honking of horns, the wailing of sirens, the rumbling of subway trains. Not to mention the hustle and bustle of millions of people. I strain my ears, but all I hear are the rustle of tree leaves and the faint buzz of a single bee in the grass. Where are all the people? Where is the action? Doesn't anyone live here?

"Where is everybody?" I ask Raymond.

He points down the hill at a large green building

shaped like a barn. "In the lodge having breakfast."

"No. I mean the rest of the people who live here."

Raymond looks around. For the first time I notice that our log cabin is part of a circle of log cabins spread out on the side of a hill. "Well," he says. "Probably there are about a hundred campers. And maybe twenty-five counselors. That's it."

"That's all?" This is amazing. This is strange. This is scary.

"The country is different from the city," Raymond explains. "There are fewer people and more space."

All my life I have lived right up against someone else, whisker to whisker, tail to tail. It was like that growing up with twelve brothers and sisters and twenty-three cousins in the cold damp basement of the Salvation Army Thrift Shop on Broadway. It was like that in my mouse hole in the movie theater and in our dollhouse in Macy's and on the streets of New York. I like it that way. It's friendly, and it keeps me warm at night.

"Don't they feel lonely," I ask, "with all that space?"

"I don't know," says Raymond. "I've always wanted to try it and see."

So, with a glance down the hill to make sure the campers are still eating, we step away from the cabin into a field of grass.

Of course I've seen grass before. They have it in Central Park. But I never knew there could be so much of it or that it could grow so tall. I take one step, and I am surrounded. Grass waves in my face. It tickles my ear. Everything else disappears. I am lost in a jungle of green.

"Help!" I call. "Gang, where are you?"

"Here," says Fats right next to me. He is turning somersaults in the grass. He attempts a cartwheel, but something goes wrong and he lands on his large stomach. "Grass is so soft!" he marvels.

Raymond emerges from a patch of clover. "Look what I found," he says, waving a bunch of pink flowers under my nose.

I take a whiff. My nose feels stuffy. Then it feels hot. Then it feels all tickly. *"Achoo!"* I start sneezing, and I can't stop. *"Achoo! Achoo!"* My nose is throbbing. My eyes are watering. The world is spinning.

"Take his arms," I hear Raymond say. "I've got his feet." I feel myself being carried through the grass, which tickles me at every step. *"Achoo! Achoo! Achoo!"* Then I am deposited none too gently on the ground.

For a few minutes I lie there, a heap of total misery. At last my sneezes subside into sniffles. I open my eyes. I am lying on a pile of pine needles. Above me I see gently waving pine branches and the anxious faces of Raymond and Fats.

"Are you all right?" Fats inquires.

"It seems," adds Raymond, "that you are allergic to clover."

I sit up. The grass was tickly, but these pine needles are prickly. And there is something sharp under my left elbow. I reach under and pull out a pinecone.

"I'm allergic to more than clover," I say grumpily. "I am allergic to the country."

Fats leans on his elbows and looks up at the sky. "I kind of like it here," he sighs. "It smells like Christmas all year-round."

"The peace and quiet is refreshing," agrees Raymond. "And there is so much to observe. I've read all the nature guides, but I never knew there were so many wildflowers. And birds. Already I've spotted a purple finch, a tufted titmouse, and a yellow-bellied sapsucker. No wild animals yet, though."

"Wild animals?" I hadn't thought of that. But of course there are bound to be wild animals in the country.

Raymond nods. "You know, rabbits, skunks, raccoons, deer. They all live in the woods. I don't know if they have moose in Vermont. Or bears."

Bears. Just the word sends a shiver from the top of my ears to the tip of my tail. Three mice would be a mere appetizer to a bear. Then suddenly I see in my mind another kind of wild animal. This one glides across the night sky on silent wings. Without warning, it swoops down on its poor prey and carries it off in sharp, relentless claws. I'm not sure if I have seen this creature in the movies or in my darkest dreams. Or maybe my mother warned me about it a long time ago.

"Do they have owls in Vermont?" I ask Raymond.

"Absolutely," he replies. "Screech owls, barn owls, the great horned owl."

This does it. The dangers of the city I can handle: trampling feet, revolving doors, alley cats, exterminators, runaway taxis, traffic jams. But this is different. This dark, menacing shadow comes down from the sky.

"Gang," I say, jumping to my feet, "the country is not for us. We are city mice. We're going back where we belong."

Fats glances nervously over his shoulder. "Maybe you're right, Marvin."

"How will we get there?" asks Raymond mildly.

"We'll walk," I decide.

"Do you know how far it is? From my study of maps, I would say it must be three hundred miles to New York City."

"So it will take a couple of days," I scoff. "We can do it."

"I'm afraid it will take a little longer than that." Raymond pushes aside some pine needles, picks up a twig, and starts scribbling. "Hmmm. Marvin, would you just walk from this tree to that bush over there?"

I don't know why I am doing this, but I do it.

"One Mississippi . . . two Mississippi . . ." counts Raymond. And on and on until I reach the tree. "Good. You can come back now."

I peer over his shoulder. "If it takes one hundred and seven seconds to travel ten feet," he mumbles, "and there are five thousand two hundred eighty feet in a mile . . ." He scratches furiously in the dirt. "Multiply by three hundred . . . divide by ten . . . I've got it!" He looks at me with the satisfaction of a math problem well done. "Six and a half months. And that's without stopping to eat or sleep."

"Six and a half months!" I exclaim. "It will be winter by then."

"You can't walk," says Fats, "if you don't eat." He sits down again.

My brain is racing, searching for a new idea.

"I know," I say suddenly. "We'll hitchhike."

I can see it all now, just like in the movies. We

stand at the side of the road, the wind in our faces, our thumbs out. And soon a friendly truck driver picks us up. We sit high on a comfortable seat, munching on doughnuts and watching the headlights pierce the darkness as we speed through the night.

"Marvin." Raymond is looking at me, a tiny frown furrowing his forehead. "I think you're forgetting something. We are mice, not men."

Abruptly my fantasy switches. We stand at the side of the road, the wind in our faces, our thumbs out. Cars and trucks speed by, but no one stops. No one sees three poor little mice shivering in the cold. Or worse yet, a truck driver does see us and swerves to run us down.

I shiver in the heat. "Well," I say, "maybe not. But don't worry, gang. There has to be a way. Fats got us into this, and I am going to get us out." I draw myself up to my full height. "This calls for a Plan."

"A Plan!" Fats claps his paws, and Raymond nods approvingly. They love my Plans.

They wait. I wait. But a Plan doesn't spring immediately to mind.

"While you are coming up with a Plan," Raymond suggests, "maybe we should stay at this camp. Just for a few days."

I consider. While I do, I look down the hill. Campers are streaming out of the lodge building. Breakfast is finally over.

It's either camp or the woods. The woods full of wild animals.

I make a fast decision, like a real leader should.

"Gang," I announce. "We'll stay. Just for a few days."

4

I Undertake
a Scouting Mission

So we settle in, in the empty care package box under the bed in the log cabin. Just for a few days.

Fats chews two small peepholes in the side of the box, and we take turns standing guard. After a couple of days, though, I start to relax. No one comes near our hiding place. No one even looks under the bed. This is where the campers shove everything they don't want. We are safe here.

Raymond the worrier is not so sure. "We've never lived so close to humans before," he frets. "Do you realize a boy is sleeping just inches above our heads? We must be alert at all times. And, above all, quiet."

Our box is very comfortable, especially after we

remove those awful marbles and replace them with three abandoned wool socks. A sock makes a perfect sleeping bag—warm and cozy and just our size. And we have plenty to eat. Each night, after checking to make sure the campers are asleep, we creep silently from our hiding place. We scour the cabin for the leftover food of the day: a half-eaten cookie, a few potato chips, maybe the crumbs of a candy bar. And on the days when a new care package arrives, we have a feast that satisfies even Fats: chocolate-covered peanuts and caramel-covered popcorn, jelly beans and Tootsie Rolls, homemade cookies and brownies and cupcakes.

"Just take the crumbs," Raymond keeps cautioning us. "If we eat too much, the campers will notice."

Naturally, Fats eats too much. But no one seems to notice.

A few days of this and my gang is looking quite contented. Fats has never eaten so much junk food. And Raymond, who loves to collect things, has the beginnings of several new collections, all scavenged from the campers' mess. He has ten bubble gum wrappers, eight buttons, seven used postage stamps, five fishing lures, and—his own personal favorite—four baseball cards. They are in no hurry to leave, I can tell.

But I am. I still can't get used to the country, with its strange smells, its quiet that makes it hard to sleep, all that space and fresh air and everything too clean. I spend my days sneezing and my nights dreaming—of Chinese food in take-out cartons, crowds of pushing Macy's shoppers, fire trucks and burglar alarms and the subway at rush hour. One night I dream that six cops are chasing me with swinging nightsticks, and I awake with a smile. Those were the good old days.

I keep working on my Plan. Everyone at this camp, I reason, has come from somewhere else. Like us, they arrived by some kind of vehicle. If there is a way to get here, there has to be a way to get back. So I keep my ears peeled, listening for clues.

"Storm Williams *has* to be the best hitter in the National League. Look at how many home runs he has."

"But what about Will Parker? His batting average is amazing, close to .400. That makes him the best hitter."

These are the voices of the two campers in the bunk beds right above us. Their names, I have learned, are Sam and Kevin. Sam, in the lower bunk, is the boy we were sent to. He is a nut about baseball, and especially the New York Mets. It is his lost baseball cards Raymond is collecting. And his baseball cap and baseball mitt and baseball magazines that surround our box. Kevin, in the upper bunk, prefers hiking and fishing. But he doesn't mind talking about baseball. All these two do is argue—about teams and players and batting averages and other strange-sounding statistics. ERAs and Ks and MVPs. Raymond finds all of this educational, but I find it boring. And it is definitely not giving me any clues.

Not until one night about a week after our arrival. Lights are out, and a couple of the campers are already snoring. I'm a little sleepy myself, comfortably curled up in my sock sleeping bag. Sam and Kevin are still talking baseball.

"Jo-Jo Fernandez leads the league in strikeouts. It's either Fernandez or Red Murphy."

"No, it's Steve Hirshenheimer. I read it in *Baseball Weekly* coming up on the bus from New York."

New York? Did somebody say New York?

Suddenly I am wide awake. New York. Bus. This is a clue.

"Did you hear that, gang?" I say.

A tiny snore comes from Fats's sock. And Raymond replies, "I think it's Fernandez. He struck out thirteen against Pittsburgh last week."

"Fernandez Shmernandez! Didn't you hear what

Sam said? He came up on the *bus* from *New York*!"

Now I have their attention. Fats climbs, yawning, out of his sock. Raymond puts down his baseball cards. The thought of New York sends my agile brain racing into high gear. And suddenly it comes to me: a Plan.

"Men," I say, "if there is a bus from New York City to Vermont, there is a bus from Vermont to New York City. I am going on a scouting mission to find out when the next one leaves. And I'm going tonight."

Fats looks bewildered. Raymond looks alarmed.

"But, Marvin," he protests. "It's dangerous out there. You will need certain equipment: an emergency weapon, a disguise. You can't go now. Wait till tomorrow, at least."

But I can't wait, not even for a minute. I have all the equipment I need. My emergency weapon is my powerful brain, and my disguise is darkness. Besides, if I wait I might lose my courage.

"So long," I tell my gang. "Don't wait up for me."

And before they can stop me, I leap over the side of the box and am gone.

It is dark outside. The darkest darkness I have ever known. In the city at night, a little light always comes

47

from somewhere: a street lamp, car headlights, a night-light burning inside a shop. But in the country it is completely black, like the inside of a coat pocket. There is no moon tonight and only a few stars winking above the pine trees. I stand still for a moment next to the screen door, and I shiver.

What is out there, lurking among the trees? Or looking down from the sky with sharp, cruel eyes?

I cannot allow myself to think these thoughts. Instead, I remember my other emergency weapon: my speed. I go swiftly into action.

My destination, I have decided, is the building the campers call the lodge. This seems to be the center of the camp. The boys eat there, get their mail there, see movies there. This would be the logical place to find a bus schedule. Looking down the hill, I can make out a large shape, blacker than the blackness. That must be it. And my sharp eyes spot some smaller shapes: a rock, a tree stump, a clump of bushes. Using these shapes as cover, I calculate the fastest route down the hill.

And then I'm off. Zip—I dart from the cabin to a nearby rock. I pause to look and listen. If anything is watching, it won't catch me. I am faster than a speeding taxi, slipperier than a sewer rat, craftier than an alley cat. With my city smarts, I can outrun any mere wild animal and outwit him too. After all, I am Merciless Marvin the Magnificent.

Zip, zip, zip—I go from rock to tree stump to rock. And then to a round bush that could hide an army of mice. One more zip, and I am there.

Diving beneath a tree root, I gaze up at this lodge. It is large, not tall like the skyscrapers I know in the city, but wide. It is constructed of stone and wood, with a huge chimney at one end. Old, I would say, but solid. This does not scare me. I am an experienced hand at getting inside buildings. No matter how formidable they look on the outside, I know somewhere I will find an opening just big enough for a mouse to slip through.

Sure enough, as I creep toward the door, I spot it. The door is made of heavy, dark wood. But beneath it runs a long crack. A Fats full of Tootsie Rolls might not fit. But I take a deep breath and think thin, squeezing my bones until my stomach touches my spine, and—zip—I am inside.

I find myself in a hallway. By the dim yellow glow of a night-light, I can make out a huge room to my left, with shadowy bumps of furniture and a fireplace at the end. To my right is a phone booth and beyond it a smaller room. I see the outlines of desks, chairs, and filing cabinets. This has to be the camp office. What more likely location could there be for a bus schedule? I decide to investigate.

Like the master detective I am, I comb every inch of that office. I inspect piles of papers. I slip in and out of desk drawers. I flip through the Rolodex. I even check the wastebaskets. But all I get for my efforts is a wad of chewing gum tangled in my tail.

And then, coming out of the office, I see it. A bulletin board. Stuck on it with tacks are a bunch of slips of paper. One of them is the bus schedule, I just know it.

Immediately one paper catches my eye. On one side is a long column of numbers: "8 A.M., 9 A.M., 10 A.M." This is it: a schedule! It looks like there are a lot of buses to New York City. I glance at the next column. I can't quite make out the words. For a moment I wish I'd listened to Raymond and brought equipment. A flashlight would come in handy right now. Raymond the Reader would come in handy right now. Sound it out—that's what Raymond would say. I stare at a word that looks vaguely familiar. "L-uh," I sound out. "Luh-n . . . Lun-ch!"

It is a triumph of reading, but it leaves me puzzled. Why is lunch on a bus schedule? Then I recognize another word from Raymond's card collection: "baseball." And I sound out another: "sw-im-ming." Suddenly it dawns on me. This is not a bus schedule. It is a camp schedule.

"Rats," I growl. Maybe there is no bus schedule. Maybe there is no bus to New York City.

But I have come too far to give up now. I am not leaving until I have combed every inch of this lodge.

So I steal across the hallway into the big room. This room is almost as dark as the night outside. The only light comes from the fireplace, where the last coals of a fire glow faintly red. As I move closer, the bumps of furniture become couches and chairs and Ping-Pong tables. Over the fireplace are more antlers, only these are giant size. I stare up at them. Antlers this enormous could only belong to a moose, I decide. Of course: Camp Moose-a-honk.

In front of the fireplace is a dark, shaggy fur rug. Could it be a bearskin? I creep closer. It is as big as a bear. It is shaped like a bear. Cautiously I reach out a paw to touch it. The fur is as thick and soft as a bear's fur should be.

Sinking down into its softness, I stretch out in front of the fire. This is the life. It is cozier even than my sock sleeping bag. Wait until I tell Raymond and Fats about my encounter with a bear.

And then the rug moves. Up—and down. Up—and down.

My sigh of contentment becomes a shudder of horror. This is no bearskin rug. It is a real live bear!

A second later I am running for my life. The bear is awake. With a growl of rage, he comes after me. I dart behind a chair, then take three turns around a table leg, but I cannot shake him. I can feel his hot breath, his vicious fangs only an inch from my tail. He is gaining on me. With a last desperate burst of speed, I dive beneath a couch.

The bear's powerful jaws snap shut on empty air. Though he claws and scratches, his terrible snout will not fit under the couch. For the moment, anyway, I am safe.

I listen to his growls of frustration. He sniffs. He whines. He barks.

Barks?

I look again at his terrible snout. On closer inspection, I see whiskers, a moist black nose, a full set of sharp white teeth. But no vicious fangs. This is not a bear. It is a plain old domestic dog.

Bear or dog, he seems determined to eat me. Ducking out the back of the couch, I make a run for the door. But he cuts me off at the hallway. This is a young dog in top condition. Well, I am in top con-

dition too. And I still have a few tricks up my sleeve. Scurrying up the leg of a Ping-Pong table, I leap over the net a few times to taunt him. Then I toss a paddle over the side. As he chases it, I jump down the other side and am off again.

I lead him on a merry chase, into another room, filled with long tables and chairs. This must be the dining room. I hear the dog's toenails clicking on the bare floor as I weave in and out of chair legs, always one step ahead of him, searching for another way out of this lodge.

Ahead of me, I spot a door. Darting through it, I find myself in a kitchen. It is a large square room, filled with gleaming metal: stoves and refrigerators, counters and cupboards, walls of tall shelves. There is nothing to hide behind in this slick, slippery place, nowhere to go to escape that pesky dog, who is still hot on my heels. I have only one choice. I go up.

Up a counter, up a cupboard, up a set of shelves to the very top one. On this shelf sits a mixing bowl. Using all my strength, I just manage to pull myself up over the edge, and tumble down inside.

I am safe. He can never reach me here. As my hammering heart slows to its normal speed, I hear him whining, talking to himself about the unfairness of the situation. Will he settle down to wait? I wonder. But he is a young dog, with little patience. Soon he hears something, or perhaps he remembers the comforts of the fireplace. Click, click. His toenails go out the door. The kitchen is quiet.

I have triumphed again. Now all I need to find is a crack leading outside, and I am home free. But as I'm about to jump down, my sharp ears detect another noise. It is a rustle so small it is hardly a sound at all.

Something is familiar about it. I lift my eyes over the rim of the bowl, and blink in amazement. Is it possible? Can this be? There, bustling about in the shadows, is another mouse.

In a moment I am out of my hiding place and down on the floor.

"Psst!" I tap this mouse on the shoulder.

He jumps. "Oh my goodness, oh my dear," he sputters. "What a start you gave me."

"Sorry," I say. And then I introduce myself. "I am Merciless Marvin the Magnificent."

He stares at me, his whiskers twitching nervously. "Glad to meet you. Yes, very glad, I'm sure. My name is Ellsworth J. Peabody III. Of the Peabodys who live in the meadow."

"The meadow?" I repeat. "You mean you're not visiting? You actually live here?"

Ellsworth J. Peabody III looks puzzled. "Why, certainly. The Peabodys have lived in the meadow for generations. And a wonderful place to live it is too. Full of warm sunshine and sweet grass, tasty seeds and juicy berries. What more could a field mouse want?"

Now it is my turn to stare. Raymond once read to me from his nature guide about field mice, distant cousins of ours who live in holes in the ground and survive on a diet of seeds and berries. A poor excuse for a mouse, I thought at the time. And here I am face-to-face with one.

"If you're so happy in the meadow, what are you doing here?" I ask.

"Ah," sighs Ellsworth. "It's the children. They like a little change now and then, don't you know? I have eight of them. And tomorrow is little Matilda's birthday. I promised her some Honey Sugar Oat Bran Puffs as a treat."

"Honey Sugar Oat Bran Puffs? What are they?"

"If you will follow me," he says politely, "I'll show you."

Ellsworth leads the way to a door I hadn't noticed. Behind it is another small room. This room is filled, from floor to ceiling, with shelves. And the shelves are filled with food.

"Wow!" I exclaim. "A food room!"

Ellsworth corrects me. "They call it a pantry."

Jar after jar of peanut butter lines one shelf, jar after jar of jelly another. There are cans of chili and soup and spaghetti sauce, jugs of mustard and catsup, bags of hot dog buns, boxes of cereal, huge sacks of flour, sugar, and rice. These are not exactly my favorite foods. Still, with a pantry like this, a mouse could never starve.

Ellsworth stops at a cereal box that seems to have sprung a leak.

"Here, Marvin," he offers. "Try a Honey Sugar Oat Bran Puff."

Round and white, it bears a frightening resemblance to those awful packing marbles. Hesitantly, I take a bite. It is healthy-tasting, like the sunflower seeds I tried once in Macy's health food department. Yet sweet.

"Not bad," I decide. "Not bad at all."

So Ellsworth and I settle down for a midnight snack. While we are munching, he asks, "And which meadow do you come from, Marvin? Across the lake? Over the mountain?"

"Across the lake and over many mountains," I reply. "And rivers and highways. I am a city mouse. From New York City, to be exact."

"Oh my goodness, oh my dear!" His eyes open wide. "I had an uncle once who visited New York City. Great-uncle Sidney. He was an odd mouse. Only a Peabody by marriage, you know. He loved to travel.

Oh my, the stories he told—of buildings so tall you can't see the tops of them and trains that run under the ground, and so many people doing so many things that they never stop to sleep. A strange place, I thought. All that noise and dirt and grime! You must be glad to be out of there."

"Glad?" I am indignant. "New York City is my home. I can't wait to get back to that noise and dirt and grime."

His eyes open even wider. I tell him then how I happen to be here. I describe my gang and our wonderful life at Macy's. And I try to explain about New York City. The thrill of living by your wits. The excitement of something happening every minute. The parades, the parks, the theaters, the museums. The restaurants with a food for every mood: pizza, Chinese egg rolls, corned beef sandwiches with a kosher dill pickle on the side. The very thought of it sets my mouth to salivating.

All the time I am talking, Ellsworth is shaking his head. He doesn't seem to understand. Well, what can I expect? This is a mere field mouse. Probably his taste buds are satisfied with seeds and berries.

Finally I get to the question I've been waiting to ask. "So when does the next bus leave for New York City?"

Ellsworth shakes his head again. "There is no bus to New York City. Not until the end of the summer. When the first leaves turn red on the maple trees, the camp closes down. Then it is peaceful here once more."

I can't believe it. "But how can we get home?"

He thinks for a moment. "There is one possibility. The camp has a Visitors' Day. A terrible time it is. Cars parked everywhere. Mothers and fathers and little children tramping around, having picnics in the meadow." His whiskers twitch violently at the thought. "I always stay in my hole until it is over. But perhaps you might find a car going to New York City."

This is it: a new and improved Plan! Going by car is even better than bus. It's daring. It's exciting. And with me in charge, it can't fail.

I have just one question. "When is this Visitors' Day?"

"Hmmm," says Ellsworth. "I'm not just sure. Seems like it's when the blackberries near the brook start to turn ripe. And the Queen Anne's lace blooms in the meadow."

"Blackberries? A queen in the meadow?" I'm all confused.

"Don't worry, Marvin," he reassures me. "You'll know. It's when the commotion begins."

59

5

I Become a Camper

"Seeds and berries?" says Fats. "You met a mouse who *likes* living on seeds and berries?" He shakes his head in disbelief.

"What did this Ellsworth look like?" Raymond asks. "I've never actually met a field mouse."

It is the next morning, and I am telling them the story of last night's adventures. Only my gang seems more interested in Ellsworth J. Peabody III than in my new Plan.

"A normal-looking mouse," I answer impatiently. "But hopelessly backward. Now, what did you think of the Plan?"

Raymond twirls his whiskers, thinking it over.

"Well," he answers slowly. "It's an interesting idea. But there are certain risks."

Fats has a worried look. "What if we got in the wrong car? And it wasn't going to New York City? And we didn't even have any lunch?"

No vision, these two. No confidence. No daring.

"Nonsense!" I reply. "It's a brilliant Plan. With me as your leader, it can't fail." And I give them my most evil, penetrating stare.

"Uh—right, boss," stammers Fats.

"With careful planning, it just might work," admits Raymond.

"With careful planning, we might get to ride in a sports car," I add.

Fats brightens at this. Now that I have their attention, I reveal the details of my Plan. As I see it, this one is so simple, it's practically foolproof. All we have to do is locate the right car. In the commotion Ellsworth talked about, it will be a snap to sneak on board and stow away under a seat. And we will be on the road again, on our way to New York City.

As I am talking, I see my gang nodding. The only question left is the one I asked Ellsworth. This time Fats asks it.

"When is this Visitors' Day?"

"I don't know," I have to confess. And I repeat

that nonsense about blackberries in the brook and queens in the meadow.

"Huh?" Fats's mouth drops open.

"It shouldn't be hard to find out," Raymond says. "The campers are sure to talk about it."

"Exactly," I agree. "That is the beauty of my Plan, gang. All we have to do is wait and listen."

As it turns out, we don't have to wait long. We get our answer that very afternoon.

It is a rainy day. I can hear the rain pattering on the roof, smell the aroma of wet slickers and soggy sneakers. The campers are lying around the cabin, reading baseball magazines, writing letters, complaining about the rain. By now we know all their names. Besides Sam and Kevin, there are Steve and Hot Dog, who share the next bunk beds. Hot Dog receives the most care packages and is therefore Fats's favorite camper. There is Dave, who loves fishing, and Tommy, a big basketball fan. And Eric and Tim, and Mark, the owner of the deep voice. He is the counselor for Red Oak Cabin. We have also learned that, for some strange reason, all the cabins are named for trees.

"Our first real baseball game, with Camp Echo Rock, and it's called off. And I was going to play catcher too." That is Sam's gloomy voice.

"I signed up for the hike to Jake's Pond. This old hermit guy had a falling-down cabin there. But now it's been canceled." That one is Kevin.

Their moans and groans are interrupted by the slam of the screen door. "Mail call!"

The boys perk up a little. "Anything for me, Mark?"

"Toss all my letters right up here."

Fats perks up too, peering eagerly out our peephole. He is always on the lookout for a care package.

"Dave, you're in luck. Nice big package from home."

I can see Fats starting to drool.

"Letter for you, Tommy. And two for Hot Dog. One each for Kevin and Eric and Sam. That's it, guys. That's all."

There are a few groans, then the sounds of ripping envelopes and rustling paper. And a minute later Kevin's voice.

"My parents can't come for Visitors' Day. My stupid cousin is having her stupid wedding that weekend."

"Mine can," says Sam right above us. "And get this. My mom says they're bringing me a surprise. That can only mean one thing: my new catcher's mitt! They

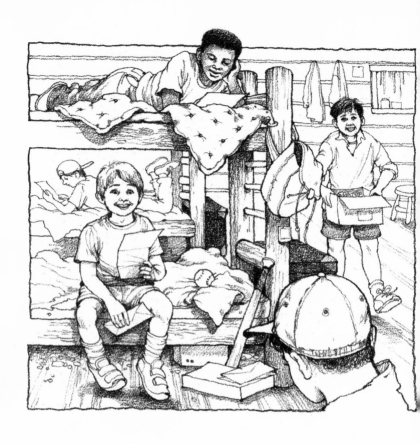

promised me one for my birthday." He starts bouncing on the bed. "Oh, wow! A catcher's mitt!"

Fats is bouncing at the peephole. "Oh, wow! Cupcakes!"

"Quiet!" hisses Raymond, grabbing him by the tail. And then I hear the magic words.

"Three more weeks!" Sam says. "I get my catcher's mitt in only three more weeks."

Three more weeks.

"That's not long," says Raymond, placidly rearranging his baseball cards.

"Not long at all," agrees Fats, wiping cake crumbs off his whiskers.

But to me, a mouse of action, three weeks is forever. What are we going to do all that time? We can't just lie around eating care packages. Three more weeks of cupcakes, and Fats won't be able to move a muscle. We have to stay in shape for our big adventure.

Then it hits me. These campers are busy just about every minute with their baseball and basketball, hiking and swimming. As long as we have to be here, why don't we try a few sports ourselves?

So it is that the next day I undertake another scouting expedition. Only this time it is broad daylight. And I take my gang along.

Because we were sent to Sam and are residing under his bed, we have come to think of him as our camper. We will follow him, I decide, and do what he does. We begin right after breakfast. As he climbs the hill from the lodge, we are waiting in the grass by the cabin steps.

"I don't like it," Raymond whispers anxiously in my ear. "I don't like it at all. Outside in broad daylight with campers all around. And no place to hide."

"There are plenty of places to hide," I reassure him. "Rocks and bushes and all this grass."

"And we didn't bring a disguise."

"We're already in disguise," I point out. "We are field mice."

He keeps on worrying. "What about equipment? We should at least have equipment."

I shake my head. "Today we travel light and move fast."

Raymond looks disappointed. He prefers an elaborate operation, full of fancy disguises, ropes and keys and can openers, and Plan A and Plan B.

"Sssh! He's here!"

Sam's feet are next to the steps. I'd know those scuffed-up sneakers anywhere. And Kevin's next to him.

"I better get going," Sam is saying, "or I'll be late for archery. See you at lunch." And suddenly he is walking away.

"Let's go!" I hiss.

We dart after him, through the tall grass. This kid walks fast. To keep up, we have to run. A couple of minutes of this and Fats is huffing and puffing. It looks like my shape-up program has come just in time.

"Run, Fats, run!" I urge.

"I'm—huff—running as—puff—fast as I can."

Raymond has him by the elbow and is dragging him along. I can barely see Sam's sneakers. Then, suddenly, they are gone. All I can see is a green sea of waving grass. Grass in front of me, grass behind. Grass to the left, grass to the right. Grass, grass everywhere.

"Help!" I shout. "We're lost!"

"No, we're not," Raymond says quietly and points. "Look." Through the grass, I can make out three brightly colored targets set up in a field. And a bunch of boys with bows and arrows in their hands.

So this is archery. We duck behind a rock to watch.

One by one the boys step up and shoot arrows at a target. Most of them miss. This takes about a minute. They spend the next fifteen minutes walking around, hunting for their arrows in the grass. When they finally find them, they get in line and do it all over again.

"What kind of silly sport is this?" I mutter, disappointed.

"Archery develops excellent eye-hand coordination," offers Raymond, the walking encyclopedia.

What do I care about eye-hand coordination? I am interested in excitement: running and jumping, climbing and chasing. This sport is all standing around looking at the grass.

"Don't worry, gang," I reassure them. "The next sport has to be better than this."

But the next sport isn't better. We trail Sam from the archery field to a small cabin in the woods. This is peculiar. What sport is played inside a cabin? From the cabin comes a loud pounding noise. Whatever it is, it sounds rough.

Creeping close to the open door, we peer inside.

Boys are hammering and sawing. They are gluing and painting. I see birdhouses and boats and bookshelves. I see belts and Indian moccasins. And a whole row of lopsided clay pots.

"What sport is this?" whispers Fats.

"It's not," I answer in disgust. "It's arts and crafts."

But after arts and crafts, Sam's day takes a turn for the better. He goes to soccer.

This is more like it. Soccer not only has running, it has pushing and shoving, falling down, and bouncing balls on heads. While Sam races from one end of the field to the other, I find a round pebble and practice some fancy footwork of my own. This is what I call a real sport.

And after lunch he has baseball. Baseball is not quite as action-packed as soccer. There is some standing around while batters swing and miss, and occasional hunting for balls. But its exciting moments make up for the boring ones. Base stealing! Inside-the-park home runs! Diving catches! Close plays at home plate! All in all, I decide, I like it even better.

Fats seems to agree. "I want to be a catcher like Sam," he decides, after watching him tag out a runner in a cloud of dust.

"I'll toss you a few," I offer, picking up my pebble.

I go into a fancy windup, then throw him my fastball.

"Oooff!" Fats misses the ball, but catches it in the cushioned backstop of his midsection. He falls over in the grass. "That hurt," he complains, looking up at me reproachfully.

Raymond helps him to his feet. "As beginners," he says, "I think we need a softer ball."

After baseball we are hot and tired. So it is a relief to find that Sam's next activity is swimming.

We follow him down a long winding path. As we round a bend, suddenly in front of us is a huge body of water. This is no mud puddle, no boat pond in Central Park. It stretches as far as I can see, deep blue and sparkling in the sun.

"It's the ocean!" whispers Fats.

Raymond shakes his head. "It's Lake Moose-a-honk."

In a moment the boys have all jumped in the lake. Some are taking swimming lessons, others are diving and splashing. And someone is in the water with them, someone big and black, with floppy ears and a waving tail. He is chasing sticks and bringing them to shore as the boys shout, "Go get it, Barney!" It is none other than my enemy of a few nights ago, the camp dog.

I point him out to my gang, and we move a safe distance away, to a spot under a bush where a tiny stream flows into the lake. It forms a perfect mouse-size swimming area. Raymond and I paddle around, cooling off, while Fats sits in the shallow water, soaking his bruised stomach.

"Come on in," I urge him, showing off my back-stroke.

"I can't," Fats says sadly. "I don't know how to swim."

After we've cooled off, we inspect the rest of the waterfront. It has a small sandy beach. And a long dock with a diving board on the end. On one side of the dock is the swimming area. Tied to the other side is a line of green canoes with moose heads painted on their sides.

"Boats!" exclaims Raymond, his eyes opening wide. "Real boats!"

"They're not *real* boats," I point out. "They don't have motors."

"A canoe is good enough for me," Raymond sighs dreamily. "Think of it, setting out across the lake on a quiet morning to see what you can see. A warm sun, a little breeze, the only sound the water dripping from your paddle."

It sounds deadly dull to me. The roar of a high-powered engine, the crash of giant waves—that would be more like it.

"Yes," Raymond goes on, "boating is the best sport."

"Boating? Best sport?" I snort. I can't believe this. "Baseball is the best sport. No contest."

"Eating is *my* best sport," Fats chimes in.

"In boating," Raymond argues, "it's just man—or, uh, mouse—against the elements."

"In baseball," I counter, "it's just mouse against mouse."

We are still arguing as we follow Sam back up the hill. The shadows are growing long, I notice. There is a grumble in my stomach. It must be dinnertime.

The boys play Toss the Wet Bathing Suit for a while, then go off to the lodge. We creep in and settle down for our own evening meal. Fats is so exhausted from his unaccustomed exercise that he falls asleep even before dessert. Raymond and I carry him to his sleeping bag.

"It's been quite a day," I say, stretching my aching muscles. And Raymond has to agree.

But our day is not quite over yet.

"Okay, guys. Get ready for the campfire," I hear Mark the counselor saying when they return from dinner.

"Campfire!"

"Hey, great!"

"Oh, boy, this is the best part of camp!"

This last was Sam. If he is this excited, I figure a campfire is something we ought to see. Besides, we've done everything else he did today. So I drag a bleary-eyed Fats out of his sleeping bag, set him on his feet, and we're off to the campfire.

We walk deep into the woods. The night is dark and the trees are tall. The woods are full of strange rustlings and stirrings. "What's that?" whispers Fats, and Raymond peers nervously over his shoulder. Trying not to think of owls, I stick close to Sam's white sneakers.

All at once we come to a clearing. Trees have been cut down and made into a rough circle of benches. In its center blazes a bright campfire. The boys gather around the fire, while we find a safe spot in the shadow of a flat rock. More and more campers are arriving, along with all the counselors. One has a guitar, and soon everyone is singing. The sound of their voices seems to fill the woods, and suddenly I'm not nervous anymore.

We stretch out comfortably on a bed of pine needles, gazing up at the stars. The songs die away, and someone begins to tell a ghost story. It goes on and on, full of fog and creaking doors and monsters that walk by night. I feel Fats move closer, clutching my tail.

"Look," I whisper in his ear.

Boys are standing next to the fire, holding long sticks. On the ends are small round white things. "Marshmallows!" breathes Fats.

The boys toast the marshmallows, then plop them on crackers. They add some chocolate and another cracker, making a kind of marshmallow sandwich.

"S'mores!" I hear Hot Dog exclaim. "Yes, this is living!"

Fats is jumping up and down. "Let me at it!" he cries.

I am forced to sit on him while I wait my chance. Finally the campers are stuffed full of s'mores. I see a little kid drop one in the grass. In a second I dart out and grab it. In another second we are having a sticky, gooey, delicious feast.

"A little sweet," I pronounce, "but not bad."

Fats's mouth is so full that all he can say is, "Mmm, give me s'more!"

Then something happens that surprises even me. A gray-haired man steps up to the campfire. ("It must be the camp director," whispers Raymond.) "Attention, boys," he says. "Since tomorrow is July fourth, we have arranged a special treat for you."

For a moment everyone waits. And then the sky above us seems to explode. Bang! Pop! Whoosh!

Colors light up the darkness: bright red, white, and blue. Shooting stars burst, pinwheels dance, rockets explode. Great showers of stars seem to fall on the treetops. And all the while there is the sound of heavy artillery, louder than any war movie. Whish! Bang!

Fats is cowering beside me, holding his ears. But in a flash of light, I see him suddenly smile. "It's fireworks!" he shouts. "Hooray!"

Next to cheese, and maybe pickles, a good noisy fireworks show is his favorite thing in all the world.

Then Fats the Fuse is leaning close to me, yelling in my ear.

"I like camp," he says.

6

I Take
a Spin in a Canoe

Our shape-up program goes into high gear the next day when Raymond, out prospecting for treasure under Steve and Hot Dog's bunk bed, comes back with a Ping-Pong ball.

I give it a kick. It's soft on the toes. I toss it in the air. It's light, yet bounces with a satisfying click on the cabin floor. I bounce it on my head, the way I saw the boys do at soccer, and I don't even have a headache.

"Perfect," I pronounce.

Now we can practice baseball without leaving the cabin. As soon as the boys go off each morning, we take over. The living room, with all its uncluttered space, makes a fine field. Raymond lays out baseball cards as bases. I pick out a bat from his collection of chewed pencil stubs. And soon I am slugging ground-rule doubles under the couch and home runs into the fireplace.

My gang is starting to shape up. Raymond, it turns out, is a natural-born pitcher. He spends hours aiming fastballs at a couch pillow and at night does scientific calculations to find out what makes a curveball curve. And Fats, after days of base-stealing practice, can finally run the length of the living room without huffing and puffing. It may be my imagination, but I think I see his fat starting to turn to muscle.

Then one afternoon everything falls apart.

It starts when a pack of bubble gum falls from the sky and rolls under the bed while the boys are changing clothes. The moment the boys are gone, Fats darts out to snatch it.

"Bubble gum!" he squeals. "Strawberry banana, yum!" He chews and grins, chews and grins. Then a cloud drifts across his sunny face. "Oh, I wish I knew how to blow bubbles."

All that afternoon while we practice baseball, Fats tries to blow a bubble. His cheeks puff out, his nose twitches, his whole body twists into a pretzel. And he keeps missing the ball.

"You'll never be a catcher like Sam if you don't pay attention," I warn, after he misses five in a row of Raymond's pitches.

I send him out to the outfield. He stands there chewing while balls roll through his legs and bounce off his nose.

"Wake up, Fats!" I yell.

Then I notice that Raymond too is in some kind of trance. His fastball is slow and his curveball is straight, and he doesn't even seem to care. He keeps looking over his shoulder.

"What's going on here?" I demand, after taking a mighty swing at a ball miles out of the strike zone and missing.

"There's a canoe on top of the fireplace," Raymond informs me.

"Don't be ridiculous!" I scoff.

"It's only a small one," he says. "One of the campers must have made it in arts and crafts."

I check. Sure enough, a tiny boat is sitting on the mantel.

"This I've got to see." I drop my bat and climb up for a closer look.

It is a canoe all right. A perfect miniature canoe. It is made of birch bark, laced together with stout thread. Except for its color, a light speckled tan, it looks exactly like those at the waterfront, even down to the tiny built-in seats. And it is just our size.

We climb aboard. Raymond dips an imaginary paddle into the imaginary water. "If only we could take her for a little spin," he sighs.

"Don't be absurd," I snap. "This thing probably wouldn't even float."

"Indians made canoes out of birch bark," Raymond points out. "And they always floated."

"Anyway, we don't have any paddles," I add.

"I could make paddles," Raymond replies.

"And besides, boating is boring."

I've got him this time. Before he can come up with an answer, Fats is suddenly jumping up and down, making strange noises. *"Mmmffoop!"*

I look. Where his nose should be is a fat pink bubble.

"Fats, old boy," I say. "You did it!"

The bubble grows bigger. It covers his face.

"Amazing!" exclaims Raymond.

Now there is no Fats, just a giant bubble that fills the whole canoe.

"Blow, Fats, blow!" we both cheer.

And then, splat! The bubble bursts. And there is Fats, looking startled, with wads of pink gum dangling from his whiskers.

"It popped!" he wails. "My beautiful bubble!"

"It's all right," Raymond comforts him. "You can blow another one."

Fats brightens. "That's right, I can!" He peels off the gum and stuffs it back in his mouth. "Okay, gang. Watch this. Here comes an even bigger one!"

And that is the end of the canoeing discussion.

But the next day I find Raymond sorting through his collection of miscellaneous objects. "Which would work better, I wonder," he mumbles. "The plastic knife and spoon or the Popsicle sticks?"

"Better for what?" I ask.

"Paddles," he replies.

The next day I find him whittling away at a Popsicle stick with a borrowed Boy Scout knife.

"What are you doing?"

"Making paddles."

I'm beginning to think he is serious.

Raymond works for several days, shaping his paddles, filing them smooth with a nail file. When they are finally finished, he tries one out in the bathroom sink. "It works!" he announces triumphantly.

Something tells me what happens next. Raymond is going to use these paddles whether I go with him or not. I can't have that. After all, I am his leader.

"Okay, okay," I give in. "We'll go canoeing."

It takes Raymond two more days to complete his preparations. But at last he is ready. Out of a torn jeans pocket, Sam's broken shoelace, and some safety pins, he has fashioned a knapsack. Into it he packs the Boy Scout knife, a compass, a pocket flashlight, more safety pins, a ball of string, two rubber bands, some bubble gum, a balloon, and a picnic lunch consisting of three potato chips, half a cookie, and some M&Ms, all wrapped up in a paper napkin.

The knapsack is so heavy he can barely stand up.

"You could leave out the flashlight," I suggest. We are making this expedition at dawn, when, Raymond says, the lake is always calm.

Raymond looks shocked. "What if we get stranded on a desert island?" he asks. "We'll need to signal for help. No, all this equipment is necessary."

The moment the campers are out the door for breakfast, we are out from under the bunk bed. And the very next moment, we are putting Raymond's equipment to use.

"Slip the rubber bands around the ends of the canoe," he directs. "Now attach the string to that safety pin. That's it, Fats. Now, very slowly, we lower the canoe to the floor."

It works perfectly. A few moments later I am

walking through the still-wet grass with a canoe balanced on my head. Fats follows, carrying the paddles, and Raymond and his knapsack stagger on behind.

"What a morning to go canoeing!" he exclaims happily. The sun is streaming through the trees. The air is still. Hardly a ripple disturbs the silvery surface of the lake.

I set the canoe down. Raymond carefully arranges his knapsack, adjusts the seats, places a paddle in front and a paddle in back.

"There," he says. "We're ready to launch. On the count of three, everybody push. One . . . two . . . three!"

Using all the power of our shaped-up muscles, Fats and I give a mighty heave. The canoe slides smoothly into the water. And sinks.

"It's going under!" yells Fats.

I grab the end just in time and drag it out of the water.

"I knew this thing would never float," I tell Raymond. "What can you expect from a canoe built in arts and crafts?"

But Raymond seems unperturbed. He rummages in his knapsack and finds a slightly damp stick of bubble gum. "Have some, Fats," he offers. Fats grins and starts chewing. Raymond walks up and down. "Ah," he mutters. "I think I see the problem. Fats, may I have just a tiny piece of your gum?"

He applies a bubble gum patch to the bottom of the canoe. "Another piece, please."

"I won't have enough to blow bubbles," objects Fats.

A couple more patches, and Fats is out of gum. But the canoe is floating.

"One more thing before we go on board." Raymond takes a long yellow balloon from his knapsack. He blows it up like a sausage, then ties it around Fats's waist.

"What's that for?" asks Fats.

"That is your life preserver," says Raymond.

Fats in a life preserver is fatter than ever. Raymond and I have to lift him into the canoe. This boat is tippy. It almost capsizes several times, but finally we get him wedged in. Then Raymond climbs in the front seat and I climb in back. We dip our paddles into the water. We are doing it. We are canoeing!

Dip and splash, dip and splash. There is nothing to this paddling stuff. Our little craft cuts through the water just like an Indian canoe.

"Uh—Marvin," says Fats, "how come we're not going anywhere?"

I look up. This is odd. By now we should be halfway across the lake. Then I realize something kind of embarrassing. We are paddling around in circles.

"Uh—Raymond," I say, "is there something we should know about steering?"

Raymond looks back. "Oh my, I forgot to tell you. If you want to turn left, you paddle on the right side. If you want to go right, you paddle on the left."

It's a crazy steering system, but after a few minutes I get the hang of it. And finally we leave our little beach behind.

It is, as Raymond said, a perfect morning for canoeing. We glide across the still water, watching rocks and pine trees pass by. The only sound is the water dripping from our paddles. It is nice, I have to admit. Dull, but nice.

At first we stay close to shore, in case of an emergency. But as our confidence grows, we venture farther out. Now the lake is a deeper blue, and tiny waves ruffle its surface. This is more like it. This is beginning to feel like an adventure.

It is then that I see something straight ahead of us on the horizon. It is round, yet flat. It is made of rocks, with a single pine tree sticking up in the middle.

"Gang," I say casually, "how would you like to eat our picnic on an island?"

"Oh, goody!" cries Fats. "Where is it?" He stands up to see better.

Our canoe starts swaying and rocking.

"Sit down, Fats," warns Raymond.

But now he is bouncing and pointing. "I see it! I see it!"

"Fats, control yourself," I order.

Suddenly his paws are waving wildly in the air. "Help!" he cries. "I'm falling!"

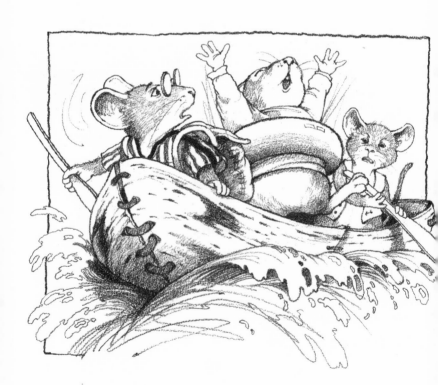

I reach out and grab him by the tail just as he is about to topple overboard.

"Never," says Raymond, *"ever* stand up in a canoe."

"Sorry," whispers Fats.

We paddle on. The island grows closer. Now we can see it clearly, shining in the sun. It is a small island, just three or four rocks and the little pine tree. But it is big enough for us.

"We'll have our picnic in the shade of the tree," Raymond decides.

"You did say you brought potato chips, didn't you?" says Fats. "A picnic isn't a picnic without potato chips."

Just as he says the word, I feel our canoe rock again.

"Fats, stop bouncing."

"I'm not." He looks insulted. "I can say *potato chip* without moving any part of my body. See? Potato chip, potato chip, potato chip!"

The canoe rocks again.

"Fats—" I start to say.

Then something seems to rise up beneath our canoe. I hear a loud splash. I catch a glimpse of shimmering fins, a flopping tail. And a giant creature leaps out of the water.

"A sea monster!" I yell.

Everything goes flying. I hit the water. Down, down,

down I go, to the bottom of the lake. I have to get up, to air. I fight my way back, through clouds of shining bubbles. At last I reach the surface.

Water is everywhere, in my eyes, filling my ears, clogging my nose. Blinking, I look around. But all I can see is water. There is no sign of my gang or the canoe or the terrible creature. I am alone in the middle of the lake.

"Look, Marvin," squeaks a voice behind me. "I'm swimming!"

There is Fats, lying on his back with his stomach in the air.

"Where is your life preserver?" I ask.

"It sank," he says, smiling. "But I floated."

Raymond swims into sight, pushing our canoe. "One paddle is missing," he reports. "But my knapsack is still here. Isn't that amazing?"

"Amazing," I agree.

And then, without warning, the water begins to churn again. A wave splashes over my head. This is like an earthquake, a storm at sea, a tidal wave. I look over my shoulder, and there is the creature heading straight for me.

I see its tremendous jaws. And its awful staring eye.

"A shark!" I gasp.

And then everything goes black.

Dip and splash. Dip and splash. I seem to be riding in a canoe. Above me the sun is shining. The sky is perfectly blue. The only sound I can hear is the water dripping from the paddles. I have never felt so peaceful. So this is what it's like to be dead.

"I think he's awake," whispers Fats.

"Marvin?" Raymond touches my tail. "Are you all right?"

I close my eyes, then open them again. I am still riding in a canoe. Raymond is paddling. "What happened?" I ask.

"You fainted," he explains.

"And I rescued you," Fats puts in proudly. "I can swim, you know."

Me, Merciless Marvin, tough guy, fainting? Being rescued by Fats, of all mice? This is embarrassing. This is not the way it's supposed to be.

But then I remember the creature. Maybe fainting was a clever maneuver. Yes, probably fainting saved my life.

"That terrible creature," I shudder. "It was trying to eat me."

"Actually, it was trying to eat a dragonfly," Raymond corrects me. "You just got in the way."

"What was it, anyway?" I ask. "A shark? A sea monster?"

Raymond shakes his head.

"The terrible creature," he says, "was a trout."

7

I Face an Emergency

Now the countdown begins.

" 'Thirteen more days until Visitors' Day,' " Raymond reads aloud from a letter from Sam's mother, which has somehow drifted under the bed. " 'Your father and Sara and I can hardly wait.' "

"Ten more days until Catcher's Mitt Day!" Sam tells Kevin.

"Eight more days until D-Day," Mark the counselor announces. "You guys better start cleaning up this cabin."

I call it Escape Day, and I am counting too. It's time to get away from this land of killer trout.

Seven more days. Six. Five.

"Only four days to go," I hear Mark say one morning, "and this place is still a disaster area. I'm going to have to declare a Clean-up Day. Starting right now."

"Uh-oh," mutters Raymond. "I don't like the sound of this."

The campers don't either.

"Hey, Mark, give us a break," protests Steve.

"My parents won't notice," argues Tommy. "It looks just like my room at home."

But Mark will not be moved. "Sorry, guys. We've got to do it."

"You know, suddenly I don't feel so good. Maybe I'm sick."

"That's not going to work, Hot Dog. Out of bed."

There are groans and sighs. And, a few minutes later, a series of strange new noises. Swish. Clank. Clunk.

Raymond hurries to one of the peepholes. "They've got brooms," he reports. "And mops and buckets. I don't like the looks of this."

"Get out of the way, Tim. Coming through!"

"Hey, watch where you're sweeping."

"Too bad, Mark. You'll have to do the mopping. I don't know how." There are hoots and whistles, clanging and banging.

It occurs to me that this is the commotion Ellsworth was talking about.

"I knew it was too risky living here." Raymond is nervously twirling his whiskers nonstop. "What if they decide to clean under the beds?"

"Ha!" I snort. "That would never happen."

"Under the beds is where they keep things," adds Fats. "Like a closet."

"Hey, you guys," booms Mark's voice. "This place is starting to look good. Be sure you get those spiderwebs over the windows. And clean under the beds."

"Under the beds?" all of the campers chorus in disbelief.

"Under the beds?" My gang and I look at one another in horror.

For a moment we are paralyzed. Then Fats squeaks, "What do we do now?"

Swiftly I take charge, like a true leader should. "We'll make a run for it," I decide. "If we can just get to the woods, we can hide out there. Somehow we'll survive. We'll live on seeds and berries, like Ellsworth."

"But, Marvin," Raymond interrupts. "Look out there. We'll never get out from under this bed alive."

I glance out the peephole. Raymond has a point.

Not only are we outnumbered, but we are up against a formidable battery of weapons: broom handles and dustpans, mops and buckets.

"What do you suggest?" I ask him.

"There is only one thing to do. We stay where we are. If we're lucky, they won't open this box, just throw it away. Then we can escape from the garbage."

As usual, Raymond's suggestion is unimaginative, unadventurous, and undaring. As usual, it makes sense. Especially with the scratchy sound of brooms advancing toward us.

I check the peephole once more—and see an enormous hand reaching under the bed.

"Hang on, gang!" I warn. "We're going traveling."

Our box is nudged, pushed, and shoved. It is turned upside down. Finally it is lifted and carried. We cling to one another, trying to remain calm. After all, we've been through this before.

This time it doesn't last long. We hear the screen door slam, then catch a whiff of outdoor air. "Stack all that junk in a pile," directs Mark. "We'll get rid of it later."

"Junk?" repeats Fats indignantly. "He calls us junk?"

Our box drops with a thud, we bump heads, and it is over.

I listen for a moment, making sure the coast is clear. "Okay, gang," I say. "This is it. Evacuation!"

In the old days in the movie theater, an evacuation of our mouseholes took us just thirty seconds. That was when the Exterminator, with all his evil potions, came to call. This one takes longer. Raymond can't leave without his collections. Fats can't leave without checking every candy wrapper to make sure we've left nothing edible behind. And when we are finally safely concealed under the cabin steps, Fats wants to go back.

"You can't do that," Raymond objects. "It's too dangerous."

"I have to," he says. "I forgot the Tootsie Roll I had hidden in my sleeping bag."

Raymond and I are forced to restrain him.

All that day we remain in hiding, while the commotion continues above us. We hear a lamp crash as the cleaning squad attacks the living room. A major water fight breaks out when they reach the bathroom. And the pile of trash outside grows taller and taller.

Finally Eric and Tim emerge, carrying a plastic bag. They dump the trash inside, tie it up, and carry it down the hill.

"There goes our little house," Fats says sadly.

"It was a nice little house," remarks Raymond. "Not fancy, not fully furnished, like our dollhouse. More like a cabin really. But cozy."

"Now it's gone forever," sniffs Fats. "Where will we sleep tonight?"

I hadn't thought about that. But already the afternoon shadows are growing long on the hill. Soon the sun will set behind the mountain.

"We can't go back inside," Raymond points out. "With everything so neat and clean, there's nowhere left to hide."

This is true. Contrary to popular opinion, a mouse's worst enemy is not a cat. It is a clean house.

"Gang," I tell them. "It looks like we camp out tonight."

Under a corner of the cabin we discover an abandoned chipmunk hole. The accommodations are not quite what I'm accustomed to. It is barely big enough for three. The walls are made of rock and the floor is bare dirt, with some old dried grass as a rug. And there are no windows at all.

"It's a bit primitive," observes Raymond. "But at least it's a roof over our heads."

Thinking of wild animals, I have to agree. The three of us curl up in a pile and are soon asleep.

But not for long. Camping out is cold. Camping

out is damp. Camping out is hard on the bones. I toss and turn, trying to get comfortable. But every time I move, I feel a pebble under my tail or Fats's elbow in my ear. It is the worst night of my life.

I wake up the next morning, stiff and aching, with a cold in my nose.

"Never again," I vow to my gang. "Take me back to civilization. Or at least inside."

We've got to find a way to move back into the cabin. As soon as the campers leave for breakfast, we creep in for a look around.

At first I think we've got the wrong cabin. Everything is in its place. The couch pillows are on the couch, the lamp shades are on the lamps. And everything is clean. The wastebaskets are empty. In the bathroom, the floor shines and the sink has miraculously changed color from gray to white.

This is amazing. This is worse than I expected.

"Marvin, you have to see this," calls Raymond.

Looking in the doorway of the bunk room, I can't believe my eyes. The clothes that used to be everywhere have been put away. Knapsacks, canteens, and fishing poles have disappeared. All the sports equipment is neatly stacked in one corner. You can actually see the floor.

I peer under Sam's bunk bed and my heart sinks.

Except for four hiking boots lined up in a row, the floor is bare. No baseball cards, no dirty socks, no candy wrappers. Not even a dust ball. Raymond was right. There is nowhere left for a mouse to hide.

This is depressing. This is an emergency.

"Gang," I say, "due to circumstances beyond our control, we can no longer live under Sam's bed. And I refuse to spend another night in a chipmunk hole. This calls for some serious thinking."

There is silence while we all put our brains to work. Raymond paces, furiously twirling his whiskers. Fats sits staring into space. My agile brain races from one idea to another. The rafters? Too high. The fireplace? Too sooty. The wastebasket? Too humiliating.

"Tootsie Roll," says Fats softly.

I stare at him. "What?"

"I could think better if I had a Tootsie Roll."

"Oh." Some help he is.

More silence.

"Sam's hiking boot!" exlaims Fats. "That's it!" And before I can say a word, he has scaled the laces and dropped down inside. A moment later I hear his muffled voice. "Get me out of here!"

I reach in and haul him out.

"It's dark down there," he says morosely. "And cramped. And it smells funny."

Raymond goes back to his pacing. I go back to racking my brain. Fats goes back to mumbling about Tootsie Rolls.

Suddenly I notice that Raymond has paced out from under the bed.

"Raymond?" I call. "Where are you?"

"Here," comes a faint voice.

I follow it to the head of the bunk bed. Stuffed into a narrow space between the bed and wall is a battered green knapsack. It has NEW YORK METS written on it in ballpoint pen, so it must be Sam's. Standing on it, peering down inside, is Raymond.

"As temporary living quarters, this might do," he says thoughtfully. "It is roomy. It has a flap that opens and closes for easy access. And extra storage compartments for my collections. There is a nice warm sweater to sleep in. I've checked, and there are no objectionable odors."

I drop down for a look around. After the chipmunk hole, this place looks like a palace. "We'll take it!" I tell my gang.

A wrinkle of worry suddenly furrows Raymond's brow. "It could be risky, though. What if the campers go hiking?"

I am willing to take that risk. It's only for three days. After that we'll be on our way home.

"If the campers go hiking," I tell him, "we do a fast evacuation."

By the time the boys return from breakfast, we are comfortably settled in Sam's knapsack. By lunch-time, Raymond has arranged his collections to his satisfaction. We are free to spend the afternoon in a leisurely game of baseball. And by dinnertime, we are facing a new emergency.

In this newly neat and clean cabin, there is nothing to eat. No leftovers from care packages. No dropped pretzels or popcorn or potato chips. Not even a candy wrapper or a cookie crumb. Nothing.

This is more than an emergency. It is a full-fledged crisis.

"What are we going to do?" whimpers Fats, a tear rolling down his plump cheek and plopping onto his well-fed stomach. And Raymond's brow is again creased with worry.

"Gang," I tell them, "we have two choices. We can go into the woods and forage for seeds and berries. Or we can raid the kitchen."

This is no choice, I realize. I decide for them.

"Gang," I say, "tonight we raid the kitchen."

8

I Raid the Kitchen

"This is going to be a snap," I tell my gang.

We are standing by the screen door late that night.

"Remember, just do what I do. Stay together. And most important, be fast!" I look meaningfully at Fats. "Ready?"

He crouches down as if he's about to steal a base. "Set?"

Raymond adjusts the straps of his knapsack. "Go!"

And we are off into the darkness.

Just like before, I dart from the cabin to a nearby rock. Raymond and Fats are right on my heels. So far so good.

Just like before, I plot our route down the hill. "That tree stump next," I whisper. "Then the pointed rock, the fat bush, the flat bush, and that twisted tree root."

But something is not just like before. I can see our route as clearly as if it were daylight. Looking up, I notice a bright silvery moon just rising over the treetops.

My first thought is that this makes our raid even easier. If we can see everything, there will be no chance of Fats tripping over his tail or tumbling down a chipmunk hole. My second thought is if we can see everything, everything can see us.

A shiver runs down my spine. And suddenly the night seems full of eyes. They are watching from the shadowy woods, lurking in the grass, looking down on us from the pine trees. Wild animal eyes.

Raymond nudges me. "What are we waiting for?"

I cannot fail my gang. I must be brave.

"Nothing," I snap. And without looking back, off I go again. To the tree stump, the pointed rock, the fat bush, the flat bush.

"Are we almost there?" puffs Fats.

"To the tree root, and we're home free," I encourage him.

But as I step out from under the bush, I experience that odd feeling again. I glance up at the sky. A dark shadow is passing in front of the moon. The shadow of wings.

"Run for your lives, gang!"

I make a mad dash for the tree root. It seems miles away. Now the dark shadow is falling over me. I know what it is. It is that creature of my scariest nightmares: an owl. I can sense the wings coming closer and closer. I can almost feel the terrible claws.

With a last desperate burst of speed, I dive under the tree root.

I am safe! I barely have time to realize it before Raymond tumbles in on top of me. I brace myself for the arrival of Fats. But nothing happens.

A long minute goes by. Nothing. Raymond and I look at each other. Slowly we raise our eyes over the edge of the tree root.

Moonlight shines brightly on the hillside. Everything is still.

Poor Fats. He just wasn't fast enough. All those Tootsie Rolls and jelly beans, those pretzels and chocolate chip cookies have done him in. I knew it would happen some day.

Then high above us something stirs, quiet as a whisper. I look up. Once more, wings are circling. Wings are swooping down from the sky. I grasp Raymond's elbow. "Here it comes," I whisper.

And, suddenly, here comes Fats. He is rolling down the hill, head over heels, tail over teakettle, out of control. Wings are swooping, and Fats is rolling. He will never make it. Tough as I am, I can't look. I cannot watch Fats meet his fate. I cover my eyes.

"Oooof!"

I am knocked flat. For a moment I just lie there, bruised and confused. When I open my eyes, I find the three of us lying in a tangled pile. And we are all alive.

I reach out and shake Fats's paw. "Nice baserunning," I tell him.

We are safe beneath the tree root. No eyes can see us. No wings can reach us. We can stay here all night, if necessary. But as it turns out, it is not necessary. A few minutes later, a cloud comes along and covers the moon.

In the new darkness, I am confident once again. "Gang," I say, pointing to the lodge, "there it is. The pantry."

After my experience with Barney the camp dog, I decide to play it safe. We will find a way in that leads straight to the kitchen. I dart to the front steps, then begin circling the building. We are in luck. The moon is still behind a cloud. Signaling my gang to follow, I creep around one corner, then along the foundation to another.

This should be close to the kitchen, I calculate. Sure enough, a familiar aroma tickles my nostrils. Food! Fats smells it too. His stomach begins to quiver. Cautiously, I poke my nose around the corner.

It is food we smell, all right. But food of an over-ripe, over-the-hill, past-its-prime kind. In other words, garbage. A row of garbage cans glitters in the dim light.

Fats sighs. But I am not discouraged. For I know that where there are garbage cans, there must be a kitchen door.

"This is it, gang!" I whisper. "Past those cans is a door. And behind that door is food."

Fats begins to quiver all over. "Let me at it!" he breathes.

Boldly we march around the corner. Confidently we stride past the garbage cans. And bump right into a wild animal.

It is as big as a garbage can and as black as the night. It is all furry. It can be only one thing: a bear!

I try to run, but my feet seem glued to the ground. Raymond is fumbling in his knapsack for his emergency weapon. But it is too late for running or for weapons. The animal has seen us. One swipe of its mighty paw and it's curtains for me and my gang. In spite of myself, I feel my knees shaking. Then I remember: I always promised myself that when my time came, I would look death straight in the eye.

Bravely I turn and look at him. It is then I notice that these eyes are not high enough off the ground to be a bear. They aren't high enough to be a dog. A cat maybe. But I know cats. This is no cat. What is it?

At that moment the moon comes out from behind its cloud. It shines down on a gleaming row of silver garbage cans. And a black furry animal with a white stripe down its back. A skunk!

In some ways this is worse than a bear. With a bear, we can only die. If we are sprayed by a skunk, we will want to die.

"Watch its tail," murmurs Raymond.

I nod. Somewhere I've heard that if a skunk's tail goes up, it is about to spray. Right now this one's tail is at half-staff. So I do the only thing I can think of. I start talking.

"Uh—beautiful evening, isn't it?" I don't wait for a reply, but keep babbling. "Ah, yes, just look at that moon. So big and round, it makes you feel you could reach out and touch it. And the stars too. Must be a million of them." I nudge Raymond and Fats. Slowly we start backing away. "My friends and I were just out for a little stroll, taking in the fresh mountain air. Mmm, delicious!" I sniff loudly. Out of the corner of my eye, I see what I've been looking for: the kitchen door. I give a tremendous yawn. "Well, all this fresh mountain air is making me sleepy. Time to turn in, I guess. Nice running into you. Good night."

And we make a run for it.

The kitchen door is closed. Locked. Sealed up tight. For a moment I panic. But then Raymond points to a window next to it. Luckily it is ajar. And the screen is in as bad shape as the ones at the cabin. We give a push, the screen gives way, and in we tumble. Down, down we fall into the dark unknown.

I land on something hard, something prickly and tickly. "Ouch!"

Raymond clicks on his flashlight, and I see that I am sitting on a scouring pad. Fats was a little luckier. He is sprawled out on a wet sponge. We have landed in the kitchen sink.

"Gang," I say, picking bits of wire out of my tail, "we made it. Thanks to me."

Without further ado, I lead them to the pantry. As they gaze at shelf after shelf filled with food, Fats's eyes open wide with wonder, and even Raymond seems impressed.

"Let the feasting begin!" I proclaim.

We feast on crackers and oatmeal, noodles and rice. They have a dry taste, but it is a change from our diet of nothing but sweets. Then Fats discovers the Honey Sugar Oat Bran Puffs and disappears. And Raymond applies all his mechanical skills to a new challenge: how to open a pickle jar with his Boy Scout knife.

Finally he succeeds, and Fats reappears. "Do I smell what I think I smell?" he asks. "Oh, boy, pickles!"

But it is I who make the greatest discovery of the evening. Tucked away on the highest shelf I come upon something large and round and covered with a waxy black shell. I sniff. I smell. There can be no doubt about it. It is cheese.

"Gang!" I call. "You're not going to believe this!"

Quickly we gnaw through that waxy covering into its golden insides. Raymond takes a bite. "Vermont cheddar," he pronounces.

Vermont cheddar! It seems like years since I've tasted it. We attack that wheel of cheese until it is reduced to rubble, and we are reduced to lying around rubbing our overstuffed stomachs.

"Now, that was a feast!" I sigh with satisfaction.

"Very tasty," agrees Raymond.

"Filling too," groans Fats.

Then, to my astonishment, he struggles to his feet. He begins to sway. He shuffles. He hums. And then Fats is lumbering in circles, feet tapping, stomach jiggling, performing his famous cheese dance.

"Cheese, cheese!" he sings. "Oh, beautiful cheese!"

9

I Attempt a Great Escape

The countdown has counted down. The day I have waited for so long is finally here. Visitors' Day. Better known to us as Escape Day.

I awake before the sun, too excited to sleep. Lying in our warm, cozy knapsack, listening to Fats snore, I go over the Plan in my mind one more time.

It is a beautiful Plan: simple, elegant, foolproof. And without knowing it, Sam has made it even more perfect. For the past two days he has been packing a shopping bag. In it are all the clothes he thinks he doesn't need at camp: flannel pajamas, long underwear, a yellow raincoat, an odd-looking rain hat. He plans to give the bag to his mother to take home.

In this shopping bag, also, will be us.

What could be easier? What could be safer? Now we don't even have to worry about slamming our tails in the car door. And we get to ride to New York City in comfort.

I can't wait to get started. But I have to wait. First for the twittering of birds that announces the new day. Then for the sound of trumpets ("Ravioli call," Fats calls it) that announces the new day to the campers. Then for the commotion of bodies falling out of bunks, the search for missing shoes, the straightening up of the cabin for the very last time.

"I can't believe it, guys," says Mark admiringly. "This place actually looks neat!"

Finally they are off to breakfast. The moment the screen door slams, we emerge from hiding.

"Well, this is it," I tell my gang. "Say good-bye to Sam's knapsack. Say good-bye to Red Oak cabin. Say good-bye to camp. We're out of here!"

We make a farewell tour of the cabin. Raymond lingers next to the fireplace, gazing up at the little birchbark canoe.

"I'm going to miss canoeing," he says sorrowfully.

Fats finds a cookie crumb the cleaning crew missed under the couch.

"I'm going to miss care packages," he sniffs.

109

I can't stand it when they get all mushy and sentimental.

"Well, I'm not going to miss anything about the country," I snap. "Chipmunk holes, Clean-up Days, pesky wild animals. Who needs it? Come on, gang. It's traveling time."

We take up our position in the shopping bag, deep in the soft folds of the flannel pajamas. Raymond has his knapsack. Fats has a few leftover crumbs of Vermont cheddar wrapped in a gum wrapper for our lunch. This is the way to travel.

Soon we hear voices outside the cabin. Not the familiar voices of the campers, but deep voices, soft voices, high little-kid voices.

"So this is the cabin I've heard so much about."

"Look, a fireplace. And everything's so neat! Why can't you keep your room at home like this?"

"See, Sara, this is where your brother sleeps."

Sara? Is it possible? Can this be Sam's family?

Footsteps come closer. And I hear Sam's voice. "That's my bunk. I have the bottom and Kevin has the top. Hot Dog and Steve are over there. And Mark has the cot on the end."

I hear feet shuffling, little kids running, then more voices as more families arrive.

"I'm Tim's mom."

"Nice to meet you. I'm Sam's dad."

"This is Dave and Tommy and Mark, my counselor."

"Jimmy, get down from there before you break your neck!"

This is getting to be a big commotion. It's time to get out of here.

"Do it, Sam," I mutter. "Give her the shopping bag."

But instead I hear him say, "Come on, I want to show you the waterfront. And the crafts center. And the great place where we have our campfires. We'll come back here later. Oh, and Mom, thanks for bringing the cookies."

"Cookies?" whispers Fats.

"Forget it!" I growl in his ear.

The cabin quiets down as the campers go off to show their families around.

The moment they are gone, Fats begins sniffing. "Oatmeal?" he asks himself. "No, that's not it. Lemon? I don't think so. I've got it, peanut butter! Oh, wow, can you believe it? Peanut butter cookies!"

I can't take it anymore. "Go get one," I tell him.

Fats looks at me. "Do you mean it?"

"Do you think it's safe?" worries Raymond.

"Just one," I say sternly. "And come right back.

Sam will be here any minute. And when he gets here, we leave."

Fats is back in about twenty seconds, without a cookie, breathing hard and looking terrified. And we hear a woman's high-pitched voice. "I saw it, I tell you. It was some kind of wild animal! It looked like a rat."

"Now, Marjorie," says another voice soothingly. "This is the country. It was probably just a chipmunk or a field mouse."

"Rat, chipmunk, mouse! What difference does it make? Do you want your son living with wild animals?"

"I thought that's why we sent him to camp."

Their voices trail off, still arguing, into the distance, and we breathe a sigh of relief. A moment later Sam is standing next to the bed.

"It's time for the picnic," he tells his family. "And after that is the parent-camper softball game. Mom, I packed some stuff for you to take home. It's all in this shopping bag."

Suddenly the bag is lifted. And just like that, we are on our way. Out of the cabin. Down the hill. On our way home to New York City.

For a few minutes we travel swiftly and smoothly. Then I feel the bag slow down. And stop.

"Here we are," announces Sam.

"Is this the picnic?" asks a small high voice.

"Yes, Sara." Her father laughs. "This is the picnic."

The picnic is in the meadow. I can hear bees buzzing. I can smell the sweet aroma of sunbaked grass. And I can smell other things too: hot dogs and hamburgers, pickles and potato salad, hunks of juicy watermelon. Fats starts sniffing and drooling, and I am forced to hold him firmly by the ear. We can't afford to take any more chances. We are staying right where we are.

So while the campers and their families feast, we have a few crumbs of Vermont cheddar. And wait.

Little kids run around, shouting. Barney the camp dog runs around, barking. The campers have a hot-dog-eating contest, and we learn how Hot Dog got his name. ("Six hot dogs, I can't believe it!" marvels Fats.) Sam's family presents him with his new catcher's mitt, and he whoops and cheers. Then everyone sings the camp song. It's a tremendous commotion. I can see now why Ellsworth would want to hide in his hole.

Finally the picnic is over, and the parent-camper softball game begins. We listen to the crack of the bat, the plop of the ball, the cheering of the spectators. ("Go, Mr. Martinelli!" "He's safe!" "He's out!"

"No way!") Fats grows tired of it all and retires to a pajama leg for a nap. But I pace the floor of the shopping bag, my feet restless, my brain alert. Our big moment is coming, and I must be ready.

At last it comes. The softball game is over. The campers are walking their families to their cars. Our bag moves along, bumping companionably against Sam's knee.

The shopping bag stops.

A car engine starts.

"Well, Sam," says his mother's voice, "we'd better be on our way. It was a great visit. We'll see you in four weeks. Don't forget to write."

"I won't," promises Sam. "Don't forget the bag."

And he hands us to her.

This is it. We are on our way. Nonstop to New York City in our own private limousine.

But then something unexpected happens.

"Sam," his mother says, "why is your raincoat in this bag?"

"I don't need a raincoat," answers Sam.

Suddenly a hand is reaching into the shopping bag.

"Hit the deck, gang!" I hiss. The three of us make a hasty dive for the bottom.

"And your warm pajamas and long underwear?" she goes on. "I'm not taking these things home."

"I don't need them, Mom. Honest!" protests Sam. "I haven't worn any of this stuff."

He hands us to his mother again.

"Well, you should," she insists. "You'll get sick."

She hands us to Sam.

Back and forth we go, like a hot potato.

"But, Mom—"

"No buts, Sam. I know it rains at camp. You need your raincoat."

The car door slams. The engine roars to life.

" 'Bye, Sam! See you in four weeks! Have fun!"

And the car drives off down the road.

My gang and I look at one another. I am in a state of shock. I cannot believe what has just happened.

Our limousine has left without us. We are still at camp.

10

I Experience the Life of a Field Mouse

Four more weeks.

That is the first thing I think of when I wake up the next morning. Four more weeks of fresh air and greenery, wild animals and wide open spaces. The thought is so depressing, I turn over and go back to sleep.

"Marvin!" Fats's sticky whiskers are in my face. "It's breakfast time! Wait till you see the leftovers from Visitors' Day. There are peanut butter cookies and butterscotch brownies and half a bag of gumdrops. And Hot Dog's mother brought him a whole birthday cake!"

"I'm not hungry," I say, turning my face to the knapsack wall.

"Marvin!" A little later it is Raymond, tapping me on the shoulder. "You've got to see this. The cabin is getting messy again. Clothes dropped on the floor, magazines and baseball mitts kicked under the bed. Pretty soon everything will be back to normal."

"That's nice," I respond.

"Don't you want to come and see?"

"No thanks."

Four more weeks. I am thinking of sleeping for four more weeks.

Though my gang tries to tempt me with offers of baseball games and canoe rides, I refuse to budge.

All that day I mope. And all the next day.

On the morning of the third day, I am arranging the sweater sleeve, making myself comfortable for another day of heavy brooding. As I stretch out, I hear Raymond mumbling to himself. "If only . . ."

"If only what?" I inquire.

"Oh—nothing. Sorry to disturb you, Marvin."

Now he has aroused my curiosity. "Say it," I growl.

"If only," says Raymond mournfully, "I had the Queen Anne's lace, then my collection would be complete."

There she is again, that mysterious queen. "Who is Queen Anne?" I demand. "And what is she doing in Vermont?"

Raymond peers at me over his spectacles. "It's a flower," he explains. "A beautiful white flower. I've been wishing for one for my pressed flower collection, and then I saw some in the meadow. But that would require an expedition." He shakes his head. "No, Marvin. Forget it."

"I think I will," I agree, yawning. What could be more dreary than a flower-picking expedition?

Ticktock. Ticktock. Time passes slowly when you're not having any fun. For some reason, I can't seem to fall asleep. Ticktock. Ticktock. I've got to do something to pass the next four weeks.

"Okay," I say suddenly, sitting straight up. "You win. Let's go pick some flowers."

The meadow is bursting with flowers: daisies and asters, buttercups and milkweeds. And Queen Anne's lace. Raymond gathers them up in great bunches. "Oh, look!" he calls excitedly. "Black-eyed Susans!"

Flowers sure have strange names, I've noticed. They also do strange things to my nose. It begins to tickle. I begin to sniffle. Too late I realize that I am standing in a clump of clover.

"Ah-ah-ah-*choo*!"

The force of my sneeze knocks me over. And suddenly I feel the earth give way. I am falling. Down, down, I tumble into a deep dark pit.

"Help! Save me!" I cry. Then "Ooof!" I land on something soft. Something warm. Something alive.

"Oh my goodness, oh my dear. What is going on?"

The voice is familiar. "Ellsworth?" I say. "Is that you?"

"Marvin! What are you doing here?"

We gaze at each other in astonishment. And then slowly it dawns on me. This is not a pit I have fallen into. It is Ellsworth's hole.

So this is the house of a field mouse. As holes go, it is roomy. And quite comfortable, lined with soft grasses, moss, an occasional feather, here and there a bit of dandelion fluff. Still, it is dark and it smells like damp earth. And it feels closed in. I hate to feel closed in.

"Marvin? Are you down there?" calls a worried voice. A moment later, Raymond and Fats are sprawled out next to me.

I perform the introductions. "Ellsworth, meet Raymond the Rat and Fats the Fuse, from New York City. Gang, this is Ellsworth."

"A pleasure, I'm sure." Ellsworth nods. "And allow me to introduce my family. This is my wife Abigail, and little Ellsworth and Henry and Prudence and Priscilla and Benjamin and Hannah and Matilda and Ebenezer. These, children, are city mice."

Now I am aware of little field mice, gawking in the shadows.

"Do sit down," urges Ellsworth. "Let us offer you some refreshments."

So it is that my gang and I spend the rest of the afternoon in a field mouse hole. We each pull up a tuft of moss to sit on. Ellsworth and Abigail bustle about, and soon the little mice are serving refreshments.

"Very tasty," says Raymond politely.

Tasty is not exactly the word I'd use. Tasteless, dry, and hard on the molars is more like it.

"Uh—what is it?" asks Fats.

"A blend of chickweed and sunflower seeds, with just a touch of alfalfa and a few hazelnuts," answers Ellsworth. "It is Abigail's specialty."

Just as I thought, this stuff is health food.

Raymond has been peering around Ellsworth's hole. "Nice place you have here," he says, nodding approvingly. "Everything neat and clean and cozy."

Cozy is a nice way of saying crowded. I think of our dollhouse, with its separate bedrooms and can-

opy beds and everything light and airy. "Tell me, Ellsworth," I say, "why do you live underground?"

Ellsworth looks shocked. "Where else could we live?" he asks. "With so many enemies, the only safe place for a field mouse is underground."

Enemies is a subject I'm an expert in. "Who exactly are your enemies?"

"Ah, well," begins Ellsworth, "there are raccoons and possums and skunks and weasels and foxes. And owls and hawks and crows. And bobcats and house cats and dogs and human beings." He pauses for breath. "Oh, and snakes, of course. Garter snakes, black snakes . . ."

All at once the young mice are squeaking.

"Ellsworth, dear," says Abigail, "you're frightening the children."

I have heard enough. By contrast, we have hardly any enemies at all: only alley cats and dogs and people. The life of a field mouse is a hard one.

"What do field mice do for fun?" I ask curiously.

"Oh, many things," Ellsworth assures me. "We make improvements on our hole. We play games with the children: musical chairs, hide the acorn, whisker tag. And we teach them about their ancestors."

"After supper sometimes we sing songs," puts in Abigail.

"And on long winter evenings we huddle close together and tell stories," finishes Ellsworth.

"That's it?" says Fats incredulously.

"It's a quiet life," admits Ellsworth. "But we like it."

I can't believe these field mice are for real.

"But don't you ever wonder about things?" I ask. "Like what is across the brook, or on the other side of the mountain?"

"Across the brook is the pine forest," replies Ellsworth. "And on the other side of the mountain is another mountain. At least, so I've heard."

"That's just it. Don't you sometimes have the urge to go see for yourself, to explore, to see the world?"

Ellsworth looks puzzled. "Why would I want to do that," he asks, "when everything I care about is right here?"

I think I see now the difference between us and this distant cousin, the field mouse. He is satisfied with his life. I will never be. I will always be searching for something more.

Suddenly my legs have a longing for space, my nose for fresh outside air. The walls of this mouse hole are closing in on me. I can't stand living underground, hiding out from the world.

I jump to my feet. "Ellsworth, old boy," I say.

"We've got to be leaving. We have places to go and people to see. But it was nice seeing you again."

"Drop in any time," says Ellsworth.

We climb out of that dim hole up into the bright sunshine.

"Ah," I sigh happily, "that's better. Gang, let's go canoeing!"

11

I Discover the Greatest Sport of All

The next day Kevin receives a care package from his grandmother.

"Mmm, oatmeal cookies," reports Fats, sniffing. He doesn't even bother looking anymore, he has such a well-trained nose. "Cracker Jack. And cherry berry bubble gum. Not a bad haul."

"And a box!" adds Raymond excitedly. "It's the right size. It's empty. He's shoving it under the bed. This is our chance, Marvin."

So it is that we move back under Sam's bed, into another empty care package box. It's safer than the knapsack, and roomier. And, as Raymond said, soon everything is back to normal. Junk piles up around us. Now that Sam has his new catcher's mitt, his old one lies abandoned next to us, and Fats adopts it as his new napping place. Raymond devotes himself to his collections, and our little house bulges with pressed flowers, bird feathers, lanyards made in arts and crafts, Cracker Jack prizes. And his most treasured possession: a baseball card of Jo-Jo Fernandez, strikeout king.

We go back to baseball in the living room and swimming at our little private beach. And once again we take the birchbark canoe for an early morning spin. This time Raymond rigs up a sail out of a triangle of torn T-shirt, the plastic knife, and some string. As a gentle breeze sends us gliding across the water, he leans back and sighs contentedly. "Finally, we're sailing. This is the life!"

It's not the life I prefer, but I guess I can take it for a few more weeks.

One hot afternoon we are cooling off in the lake. It is one of those lazy summer days that feels like it will last forever. Fats is floating on his back, watching the clouds drift by. Raymond and I are swimming around, not going anywhere, just keeping cool. All around us are the sounds of birds chirping, boys calling, Barney the camp dog splashing into the water after a stick. The ordinary sounds of an ordinary afternoon at camp.

Suddenly I hear the roar of a powerful engine. My first thought is that I must be dreaming. I haven't heard the roar of a powerful engine since I left New York City. The sound grows louder. And something long and low and bright blue streaks by.

I can't believe it. It is a motorboat. And even more unbelievably, skimming along behind it, seemingly standing on top of the water, is a camper.

"What is that?" I gasp.

"Didn't you know?" Raymond replies calmly. "It's the oldest boys. They're water-skiing."

Now I see that the camper is attached to the boat by a rope. And under his feet are flat boards, like skis. I've heard of waterskiing, of course, but I never knew it was like this. It's so fast, so wild, so adventurous. It's like flying, only on water. As I watch, the boy behind the boat does a complete turn so he is skiing backward. A minute later he turns back and jumps over a wave. And for a moment, he *is* flying.

"Amazing!" I cheer. "Incredible! Fantastic! I have to try it!"

Raymond stops his backstroking. He stands knee-deep in the water, peering at me nearsightedly. "You can't mean that, Marvin," he says. "It's crazy. It's

127

against the laws of nature. A mouse was never meant to travel at high speeds."

"Uh-huh. A mouse was meant to rest," agrees Fats drowsily.

Maybe Raymond and Fats weren't meant to travel at high speeds. Maybe they are content paddling canoes and floating with their stomachs in the air. But not me.

"I *have* to try waterskiing," I repeat firmly. "And I'm going to. Just watch me."

I do not try waterskiing that day. Nor the next. A daring undertaking like this requires careful planning.

First, I observe the water-skiers in action one more time, taking note of their equipment, the way they launch themselves into the water, their technique for jumping over waves. Then I put my crafty brain to work. How can I reduce all this to mouse size? It is a tricky problem. Late into the night I ponder. Following Raymond's example, I draw little diagrams on the back of gum wrappers until my head is spinning.

And at last I cry, "I've got it!"

"What have you got?" Raymond asks sleepily.

"You'll see," I tell him. And I climb into my sleeping bag with a smile on my face.

The next morning I gather together my equipment. Luckily, everything I need is close at hand, thanks to Fats's philosophy of never throwing away anything edible and Raymond's philosophy of never throwing away anything at all. In Fats's pantry, I find a stick of cherry berry bubble gum and half an oatmeal cookie he was saving for a rainy day. In Raymond's collections, I discover two Popsicle sticks, a roll of fishing line, and a hook that used to attach a Boy Scout whistle to a lanyard.

"Gang," I announce. "I am ready to water-ski."

Raymond looks up, frowning, from sorting his postage stamps. "Do you have any idea how fast that motorboat goes? And what happens if you fall off in the middle of the lake? Who will rescue you?"

"I will," volunteers Fats eagerly.

"Raymond, old boy," I say, "trust me. I have a Plan."

That afternoon, as the hum of a powerful engine once more reaches my ears, I put my Plan into action. I hoist the Popsicle sticks onto one shoulder and swing the coil of fishing line over the other. My gang carries the rest of my equipment. And off we go to the waterfront.

At our little beach we set down our equipment, then crawl into a bush to survey the scene. The

129

waterfront is as busy as ever. Some of the campers are having swimming races, others are taking out canoes. At the end of the dock, a bunch of older boys are waiting their turn at waterskiing. And out in the middle of the lake, just as before, the blue motorboat with its skier tied on behind circles and turns, throwing silver spray into the sky.

"You can't do it," Raymond is muttering, shaking his head. "That boat is just too powerful."

"I'm not using that boat," I inform him calmly. "The boat I am planning to use is him."

And I point at Barney the camp dog, sleeping in the sun.

Raymond stares. His jaw drops open. He blinks. Obviously he is stunned by the brilliance of my idea. Then he looks at me. "You know," he says slowly, "it just might work."

"Of course it will work," I snap.

I explain to them then the details of my Plan, drawing diagrams in the sand with a stick, as Raymond loves to do. All my *x*'s and *o*'s and arrows pointing here and there leave Fats perplexed.

"Which one is me?" he keeps asking. "What am I supposed to do?"

I take the stick of cherry berry bubble gum and

hand it to him. "This is what you're supposed to do," I say. "Chew."

A few minutes later, everything is ready. The Popsicle sticks wait near the water. Raymond is standing by with the fishing line, the hook tied to its end. Fats is happily chewing and blowing bubbles.

I grab the half an oatmeal cookie. "Wait here, gang," I instruct them. "I'll be right back."

Once more I creep inside the bush. And from that bush to another one. And then into a clump of tall grass conveniently located a few feet from where Barney is sleeping. I can see his broad black side going up and down. I hear the gentle sounds of snoring.

I lift up a paw to test the wind. It seems to be blowing from the right direction.

"Pssst, Barney!" I whisper. And I hold up the cookie.

"Zzzzzz-who-ee! Zzzzzz-who-ee!"

This dog is sleeping soundly. He must have had a hard day keeping up with the campers.

I wiggle my way through the tall grass until I am just inches from his head. If his eyes were open, we would be eyeball-to-eyeball. For a moment I stare at the powerful jaws, the curve of a wicked-looking tooth that protrudes from his slightly open mouth.

Then daringly I step out from behind the grass.

"Barney!" I hiss. And I tweak one of his whiskers. His nose twitches. One eye flickers open.

I am dancing in front of him, holding out the cookie.

"Ho-o-o"—the powerful jaws open wide, revealing rows of sharp gleaming teeth—*"hummmmm."* The jaws close. His head sinks back on his paws. He is asleep again.

I can't believe this. Usually this dog is a motion machine. Now that I need him, he has turned into a sleeping beauty.

Well, I'll show him. Bravely I step over his giant paw. Boldly I lift up one long floppy ear.

"Barney!" I shout. And I dangle the cookie right in front of his nose.

One eye opens. Then the other. He sniffs. And suddenly he makes a lunge for the cookie.

Snap! His jaws close just an inch from my tail.

Away I go, the cookie held high. And away he bounds after me. I race like the wind, through the tall grass, around a tree trunk, into a bush. He is right behind me. I hear him snuffling in the bushes. I feel his hot breath on my neck.

This is just like the old days, when I used to lead cats and cops and irate French chefs on merry chases through the back alleys of New York. Expertly I lead him where I want him to go, tantalizing him with a glimpse of flashing tail, a whiff of tasty cookie. As I reach our little beach, I slow down. And just as he thinks he has caught me, I toss the cookie onto the sand.

This is the signal. Raymond steps forward with the fishing line. While Barney is crunching on the cookie, he snaps it to the ring on his collar.

At the same moment, I pick up the Popsicle stick skis. "Fats, the gum!"

He hands me two well-chewed wads of bubble gum. I stick the gum on the ends of my skis, then plant my back paws in it. Now I am firmly attached to my skis.

"Raymond, the rope!"

He hands me the end of the fishing line.

"Now the stick!"

Raymond picks up my drawing stick. He goes into a tremendous windup, just like Jo-Jo Fernandez on his baseball card. With a mighty heave, he tosses the stick into the lake.

"Go get it, Barney!" we all cry together.

The dog looks up. He sees the stick. For a moment he hesitates, looking around for campers. But then he can't help himself. He plunges in after it.

Suddenly my fishing-line rope grows taut. It is pulling me into the water. I hang on tight, leaning back and bending my knees as I've seen the water-skiers do. Water is splashing in my eyes. I can't see anything. All I can feel is the terrible pull of the rope. I sway. I totter. I am about to take a nosedive into the lake.

And then, miraculously, the skis are underneath me. I am standing up. I am skimming effortlessly along on top of the water.

I am water-skiing!

It is a strange feeling to be standing still, yet traveling at high speed. And it is stranger still to feel water rippling beneath my feet. Trees whiz past, rocks and sand. I can see the dock, the tiny figures of Raymond and Fats on shore. But mostly all I am aware of is lake and sky, wind and spray. This is like flying through water.

My boat slows down slightly. Through the spray I see that Barney has reached the stick. He picks it up, turns, and heads for shore. Behind him, I do a wide turn too. And then we are picking up speed again.

Faster and faster I go, my skis slicing through the water like a knife through cheese. This is easy. I feel as if I've been water-skiing all my life.

Now we are nearing the shore. I can see Raymond and Fats clearly. They are waving to me. Confidently I lift one paw and wave back.

Just at that moment, my boat slows down. Suddenly my skis are sinking under me. I pull back on the rope, struggling desperately to keep my balance. And then my boat speeds up. Somehow one ski is pointing at the sky, the other at the water. I am spinning out of control. I do a flying triple somersault, leaving both skis behind, and nosedive into the lake.

"Marvin! Are you all right?"

I open my eyes to see Fats wallowing toward me.

"I'm fine," I reassure him. The only thing wrong with me is a nose full of water.

"Don't worry. I'll save you."

"But—" I start to protest. Only Fats isn't listening. He has me in a headlock and is dragging me toward shore. My head goes under. I swallow half the lake.

"Shpptfff!" I sputter.

"I won't let you sink," Fats says soothingly. "Just lie back and relax."

I decide not to fight it. I might as well let myself be saved.

A few minutes later I am lying on the sand with Raymond and Fats hovering over me anxiously. Raymond is checking me for broken bones. "Does this hurt?" he asks. "How about this? How do you feel?"

"Feel?" I say. "I feel fine. I feel terrific. I feel like doing some more waterskiing!"

And I jump to my feet.

Barney will chase a stick as long as anyone will throw one. So Raymond warms up his throwing arm again. And off I go on another exciting ride. And another. And another.

My very last ride is the most exciting. I am zipping along behind Barney's waving tail, the wind ruffling my fur, the wet spray in my eyes. All at once, straight ahead of me, I spot a wave. This is it, I tell myself. I have to try it.

I clutch the rope tightly. I brace my feet against my skis. Just as I reach the wave, I take a giant leap. And for one brief wonderful moment I am flying through the air.

Waterskiing is the best sport. Now I know it for sure.

12

I Am Captured

That night I dream that I am flying. I glide on gentle breezes. I talk with the birds. I soar high above the treetops, above the mountaintops, until I am climbing right into the clouds. I swoop down out of the sky to the blue water below. I can do anything.

I awake with a smile on my face, eager for new adventures.

Split-splat. Pitter-pat. It is the sound of rain on the cabin roof.

"Rats!" I mutter to myself. No waterskiing today. No swimming. No canoeing. There is no reason even to get out of my sock sleeping bag. I lie there, listening to Sam and Kevin in the bunk beds above me. They are muttering too.

"Rainy days at camp are the worst."

"Yeah. You can't do any of the good stuff, like sports. All you can do is arts and crafts. I hate arts and crafts."

"Me too. Probably we'll get to make more clay pots. Or another lanyard."

"I already made one for everyone in my family, including the dog. This is going to be a long day."

It is a long day. The boys go off, grumbling, to arts and crafts. I suggest a little soccer in the living room, just for a change of pace. We warm up with some dribbling drills, then I try a few head balls while Fats does his wicked stomach ball. But before we can start a game, the campers return, wearing new lanyards. They mope around a while. Then some go off to play Ping-Pong and others to watch a movie at the lodge. But just as we are setting up goals for our soccer game, they are back again.

We dive under the bed and wait to see what happens next.

"That movie was the same one we saw last week," we hear Hot Dog complain. "And it wasn't even good the first time."

"Ping-Pong is a lame game," mumbles Steve.

"I don't care how wet it is," says Dave, "I'm going fishing. Anyone want to come?"

"I will," answers Kevin.

The two of them gather their fishing tackle and bang out the screen door. No one else seems to be going anywhere, however. Bedsprings squeak as the campers settle in for some serious moping.

"Looks like they're here to stay," I tell my gang glumly.

"No soccer game today," agrees Raymond. "I think I will go finish my statistical comparison of right-handed and left-handed relief pitchers in the American League."

"I think I'll go lick my old lollipop sticks," says Fats, drooling happily in anticipation.

I can't stand the idea of being cooped up in our care package box for the rest of the afternoon. It's almost as bad as Ellsworth's hole. "I'll stay here," I decide. "Spy a little, listen to what's going on."

Raymond immediately looks nervous.

"Don't worry," I reassure him. "I'll be quiet. I'll be alert. I'll keep my tail tucked in at all times."

So my gang climbs into our box. I stretch out comfortably in Sam's old catcher's mitt and listen.

Drip-drop goes the rain on the cabin roof. Pop

goes somebody's bubble gum. Plop goes a ball into a baseball glove. Sounds like Sam is working on his new mitt again. There is the rustling of magazine pages, the low static of a radio. "Wouldn't you know it?" groans Tim. "The Red Sox and Yankees are rained out too."

This is boring. I hate lying around doing nothing. It gives me a squirmy feeling inside.

Idly I toss up the Ping-Pong ball and catch it. I do a couple of head balls. A toe ball. A nose ball.

One, two, three, four. I bounce the ball on my nose. This is easy. Wait till I show Fats my new trick.

I think I'll try a tail ball.

Oops! Somehow my tail misses. The ball bounces on the edge of the mitt, clicks twice on the floor, and then rolls out from under the bed.

I can't believe it. One bad bounce and I've lost our ball. Not only that, but the campers may find me. Alertly, I jump to the floor, ready to leap to safety in our box.

But nothing happens. Drip-drop. Pop. Plop. These are still the only sounds. Apparently everyone is so busy moping that they didn't notice. Cautiously I peer out from behind Sam's hiking boot. Right away I spot it, a small white ball resting next to a Boy Scout canteen at the foot of Hot Dog's bed.

For a moment I hesitate. I think of Raymond's dire warnings. Then I think of the Ping-Pong ball. Without it, our baseball and soccer games are over. And I think of my speed. I can zip out and grab it and zip back under the bed faster than any of these campers can blink. For me, Merciless Marvin the Magnificent, this is child's play.

I measure the distance with my eyes. Yes, two zips should do it.

Ready, I say to myself. Set. Go!

Faster than a blink, I speed across the floor, pick up the Ping-Pong ball, and dart under Hot Dog's bed.

Drip-drop. Pop. Plop. Nobody noticed a thing. I pause for a second to catch my breath. Now to zip back.

Creak. *Boing!*

What was that noise above me? I glance up to see bedsprings sagging. Then suddenly, in the space between the bed and floor, a huge upside-down pink face appears. Its mouth is open. Its yellow hair dangles on the floor. Its enormous staring blue eyes are focused right on me.

It's a giant! It's a monster! No, it's Hot Dog.

For a moment I am paralyzed. Then it speaks.

"Holy cannelloni! It's a mouse!"

Like a shot, I am out from under the bed.

"Hey, there it goes! Catch it, you guys!"

Bodies jump down from bunk beds. Feet pound on the floor. Boys are yelling in confusion, "What is it?" "Where?" "There!"

I zip from bunk bed to knapsack, from Mark's cot to a rolled-up sleeping bag to— Uh-oh. All at once my path is blocked by a tennis racket. I turn and find a scratchy straw broom staring me in the face.

"Got him!" someone exclaims.

Obviously he doesn't know who he is up against. With the ease of long practice, I slip between tennis racket and broom. But the campers have all spotted me now. They are arming themselves with rolled-up magazines, mops, dustpans, a Ping-Pong paddle. This room is getting a little too warm for comfort.

I head for the living room, where there is more space and more hiding places. I am warmed up now. I give them my best show. Around and around the legs of the table I spin. Then over and under a few couch pillows. Behind a lamp. I make a fake toward the fireplace, then dive headfirst under one of the couches.

That ought to take care of these amateurs. I've lost them, I'm sure.

But when I poke my nose out the back of the couch, I bump smack into the crisscrossed strings of the tennis racket. I retreat. Trying the front, I come up against the spaghettilike strands of a mop. And, even more ominous, at the other end I glimpse the fat black end of a baseball bat.

I am surrounded.

"He can't get away now," I hear them chortling.

That's what they think. My brain clicks into high gear, searching for a way out. The screen door! If I could just get to it, I could lose them in the wide outdoors. Something flashes through my mind, a quotation from a sports magazine Raymond was reading last week. "The best defense is a good offense."

That's it. I'll take them by surprise. I'll hit them where they least expect it. Without pausing to think it over, I charge—right into the mop.

I am stuck in its strands. I am tangled in its twists. And then, somehow, I've popped out the other side and am making a desperate dash for the door.

"Hey, look! There he goes! Get him, someone!"

Whoosh! A mop sails through the air, narrowly missing my tail.

I'm almost to the screen door. Another few feet and I'm home free.

Then, unexpectedly, the door opens. And in step the fishermen, Dave and Kevin.

"It's a mouse!" cry the other campers. "Catch him!"

Startled, both boys make a grab for me. Dave's fingers snatch at empty air. But Kevin has a fishing net. Out of the corner of my eye, I see it swoop through the air. Swoosh! And I am caught in that net like a trout.

"Yes!"

"You got him!"

"Nice catch, Kevin!"

For a moment I dangle helplessly in the air. Then someone says, "Here. Put him in this." I am dumped into some kind of container.

It is dark. The walls are high and circular and made of slippery black metal. Right away I recognize it as the living room wastebasket. Ordinarily I could be out of a trap like this in seconds. But, looking up, I see the fishing net poised to strike again. I also see a circle of boys' faces gazing down at me. Those faces, which used to seem friendly, now appear cruel and menacing.

"What should we do with him?"

"Are you kidding?" Hot Dog's face is scowling. "This guy was living under my bed. Get rid of him."

"Yeah. We didn't come to camp to room with rodents."

This is serious.

145

All at once Sam speaks up. "But he's so small," he says quietly. "Maybe we could just take him outside and let him go."

I knew I could count on our camper to be on my side. I concentrate on looking small and pathetic.

"If we let him go, he'll just move back in," argues Hot Dog. "No, he's got to be eliminated."

This guy reminds me of the Exterminator.

Kevin has been staring thoughtfully at me. "Look at the color of his fur. And those ears. And that tail. He looks just like the picture in my nature guide. This is a perfect specimen of a field mouse."

Field mouse, ha! I want to shout. But I don't. Because I think I detect a softening in their eyes.

"Hey, maybe we could give him to Nick, the nature counselor," suggests Sam.

"Good idea," says Dave. "He could put him in a cage in the nature shack, with the snake and lizards and the blackbird with the broken wing."

Hot Dog hesitates. "Okay," he agrees.

Great. Now they want to put me on display in some kind of mini-zoo. Well, better prison than death.

"We can keep him here overnight," decides Kevin. "I'll take him to Nick first thing in the morning."

Just like that, my fate is sealed. And *I* am sealed up inside the wastebasket. Something comes down across the top, cutting off light and air, not to mention the view. Then, clunk! Something heavy is piled on top of that.

"Well, that ought to hold him," says someone.

"Yeah," answers someone else. "No way any mouse is going to escape from this trap."

Their voices seem to come from a great distance. And then, silence.

Darkness. Complete, total blackness. Steep steel walls surrounding me on all sides. And that silence. This is like my worst nightmares. I am locked up in a dungeon, helpless and alone. As the minutes go by, and then the hours, I have a terrible sinking feeling that those campers were right. There is no way in the world any mouse is going to escape from this trap.

Wait a minute. What am I saying? This is no ordinary mouse we're talking about. This is me, Merciless Marvin the Magnificent. The one with the crafty brain, the stout heart, the nerves of steel. The one who never gives up.

Just like every other tight spot I've been in, there has to be a way out of this wastebasket dungeon. And I am going to find it. The first thing to do is test the walls. I check carefully for weak spots, cracks, maybe a little rust. But unlike most of the furnishings in Red Oak cabin, the wastebasket is in good shape. Equipment: that is the next thing to consider. What do I have available to assist me in a jailbreak? I am missing Raymond and his knapsack full of useful objects. And I brought nothing with me, not even the Ping-Pong ball, which I abandoned under Hot Dog's bed. Usually a wastebasket can be counted on to provide interesting trash. But this one must have been recently emptied. Poking around its bottom, I come up with three kernels of popcorn, a wad of very old used bubble gum, and a Snickers candy wrapper, without the candy.

How can I put these few paltry items to work to make my escape? I eat the popcorn, which gives me a little energy boost. Then I pace in circles, around and around the wastebasket floor. Old bubble gum . . . Snickers wrapper . . . Old bubble gum . . . Snickers wrapper . . .

"Is that a Snickers bar I smell? Take me to it!"

Never in my life have I been so glad to hear that familiar squeak.

"Fats? Raymond?" I tap on the wastebasket wall. "I'm in here!"

"Marvin?" comes another familiar voice. "Oh, thank goodness we found you!"

Whispering through the wall, I explain to my gang

how I happen to be imprisoned inside a wastebasket. And my gang makes clear to me the gravity of my situation. "The opening is completely covered by Kevin's baseball annual," reports Raymond. "And on top of that, weighing it down, is a sneaker. Not just an ordinary sneaker. A high-top."

This is not good news. Those high-tops are heavy.

"High-top or no high-top," I tell him, "you've got to get me out of here."

"This won't be easy," comes Raymond's sober reply.

I hear some mumbling sounds, a sigh. Then silence descends on my wastebasket once more.

"Hey!" I hiss through the wall. "What's happening?"

"Sshhh," whispers Fats. "Raymond is thinking."

Minutes go by. I detect a small scurrying sound.

"Now he is walking around, looking at the wastebasket from all angles," reports Fats.

And then, so quiet that I'm not sure if I am really hearing it or just wishing I were: "I've got it!"

A moment later Raymond is describing to me his jailbreak plan. "The sneaker presents the biggest problem," he explains. "It is too heavy for us to move ourselves. But by using our brains instead of our muscles, I believe it can be done. Do you remember the cranes they use in New York City for building skyscrapers? Well, I am going to devise one right here in Vermont. Actually, it's kind of a cross between a crane and a pulley. A pulley-crane, you might call it. Anyway, it will lift up the sneaker. That is Step One. And Step Two, we will then pull you out."

I have no idea what he is talking about, and I don't even care. "Go to it, Raymond old boy!" I cheer.

There begins a series of faint mysterious noises, as Raymond assembles his equipment for my great escape. On the other side of the wastebasket wall, Fats provides a blow-by-blow account of the action.

"Raymond has a fishing rod. . . . He is setting it up with the end stuck into a knothole in the floor. . . . Now he is reeling out a lot of line. . . . He is carrying the line up the table, up the lamp, up the wall. . . . He's draping it over one of those antlers on the wall. What's he doing that for? This is weird. . . . Now he's back down again. . . . He is hooking the end of the line to the sneaker. . . . Uh-oh. Got to go. He needs my muscles to help reel in this big fish. . . . Sit tight, Marvin. We're coming to get you!"

And Fats is gone. I press my ear to the wall, listening and waiting.

"Nnnnghrrgh!" That is Fats the Fuse, grunting and groaning.

"Come on, Fats. We can do it!" That is Raymond, urging him on.

Click-click. Click-click. That is the sound of a fishing rod reeling in a big one.

Then, from directly above me, I hear the tiniest of movements. Can it be the sneaker lifting off?

I stare up, holding my breath and hoping.

And then, CRASH!!! There is a tremendous thump, some wild scurrying sounds, and total silence.

Instinctively, I dive under the Snickers wrapper. I huddle there, waiting for the worst. All I can think of is that the game is up. My gang has failed me. It's just like those old prison movies we used to watch on late-night TV at Macy's. I've had my last meal—three measly popcorn kernels—and now I await the dreaded hour of execution.

I hear tapping on the dungeon wall. They've come to get me.

"Pssst, Marvin!"

Wait a minute. That sounds like Raymond.

"What?" I whisper.

"We—uh, had a little accident," he explains apologetically. "Fats got tired and let go of the reel just at the crucial moment. The sneaker fell on the floor, and we ran for cover. But no one woke up. It's amazing. These campers could probably sleep through an earthquake. It must be all that fresh mountain air."

Whatever it is, I am grateful. I have another chance.

"Stand by for Step Two," advises Raymond. "We'll have you out of there in no time."

I stand by, ready for action. And swiftly it comes.

First, I hear light footsteps above me. Then a few whispers. And then a sound that I would know anywhere. Crunch, sigh. And suddenly I know what Step Two of Raymond's plan is. Fats is eating his way through Kevin's baseball annual.

In a few minutes I detect a crack of light in my dungeon ceiling. And I can make out the voices of my gang. "That's it, Fats. You can do it. Just a few more mouthfuls now."

"But my teeth are tired."

Crunch, sigh. Crunch, sigh. The crack grows wider. And wider. Until finally it's just my size.

Then down from the opening comes a fishing line, with a large shiny hook on the end.

"Ready, Marvin?" asks Raymond.

Am I ever. I step onto the hook, taking care to keep my tail away from its sharp point.

"Ready," I answer.

"Okay, Fats," directs Raymond. "Reel him in."

Slowly, triumphantly, I rise out of the dark depths of my dungeon into the light and air of freedom. The sun is just beginning to come up. My world has never looked so good. Raymond and Fats are grinning and cheering. My gang has never looked so good.

"Thanks, men," I say.

And we shake hands all around.

13

I Turn the Tide for the Blue Team

After my narrow escape, I am careful. I do not leave our box unless all the campers have left the cabin. When I do, I walk on tiptoe. And I jump back in at the slightest noise. I am so alert that I am driving myself crazy. But Raymond is pleased.

"Now you're being sensible," he tells me.

Sensible. Sensible is so boring. Now that I am being sensible, I have a lot of time on my hands. I doze. I dream of New York City. I listen to Sam and Kevin's endless discussions of baseball.

One morning I am listening to them droning on when I notice that this time the topic isn't baseball. "Color War . . . blue against red."

"Baseball and basketball and swimming and canoe races . . ."

"Don't forget Field Day. And the pie-eating contest."

"That's the best. Oh, boy, Color War!"

They seem excited about something. Something to do with paint.

This is most peculiar. I reach out and tap Raymond's sleeping bag. "What is going on?" I whisper.

"Ssshh!" he replies. "If we keep listening, we'll find out."

Raymond is right. A few minutes later Mark explains to the new campers, and to us, what Color War is all about. It seems that this is the biggest event of the camp season. The entire camp is divided into two teams, the Blues and the Reds. Despite its name, Red Oak cabin is on the Blue team. For a whole week, the teams compete in various kinds of contests, from sports to silly relay races to strange-sounding events like canoe-capsizing, bed-making, songwriting, and pie-eating. Scores are kept by some complicated system that I don't bother trying to understand. And at the end of the week, the winning team is announced at a giant campfire.

"Hey, this is great!" the campers are exclaiming. "I want to do canoe-capsizing."

"Can you believe a bed-making contest?"

"I can't wait for the baseball game!"

Sam is so excited, he is bouncing up and down on the bed.

"When does Color War start?" he asks.

"In three days," answers Mark.

For the next three days Sam oils his catcher's mitt, preparing for the big baseball game. Hot Dog eats nonstop, getting ready for the pie-eating contest. Tommy and Dave practice the fifty-yard dash in the living room. Kevin tries to write a song.

> *"Go, Blue!*
> *We're for you!*
> *The Red team belongs in the zoo!*
> *Pe-yew!"*

This song is not going to win, I have a distinct feeling.

And finally the big day arrives. Color War begins.

The first day is water sports. We have ringside seats at our little beach for the swimming races, diving, water polo, canoe races, canoe-capsizing. Canoe-capsizing is easy, it turns out. It is getting back in the canoe that's hard.

The next day is individual sports: archery, tennis,

the high jump, the long jump, the fifty-yard dash, a race that goes all the way around the lake. After all these events, the Red team is leading, but only by two points.

The third day is Field Day. This one we wouldn't dream of missing. First come all those silly relay races. And a giant tug of war. And after that is Sam's big baseball game. So we pack up a potato-chip-and-peanut-butter-cup lunch and follow in the campers' footsteps to the meadow.

The sun is shining. Bees are buzzing in the grass. We spread out our napkin under a shady bush and lie back to watch the action.

"Ah, this is the life," sighs Fats. He picks a plump purple berry and pops it into his mouth. "Mmmm, delicious! Marvin, Raymond, you have to try one."

Raymond tastes and chews. "It's a blackberry," he pronounces.

So these are the berries Ellsworth was talking about. I try one. There is something special about a blackberry, I have to admit, warm from the sun and perfectly ripe. Soon purple juice is running down my whiskers and dripping onto my stomach. Maybe the life of a field mouse is not all bad.

We stuff ourselves with blackberries while we watch the three-legged race and the backward race and a race where the boys climb into burlap sacks and jump from one end of the field to the other. There is a lot of yelling and cheering and singing of fight songs.

> *"Go, Blue!*
> *You know what to do!*
> *The Red team hasn't got a clue!*
> *Three cheers for Blue!"*

Kevin's song hasn't gotten much better, I notice.

After the relay races are over, the campers line up for the great tug-of-war. A line is drawn in the middle of the field. One camper from each cabin steps forward. From Red Oak, it is Hot Dog. Some of the counselors join them. They take hold of a long piece of rope, and they start to pull.

"Come on, Red!"

"Go, Blue!"

"Pull, guys, pull!"

They pull and strain and grunt and groan, but neither team can move the other one over the line.

"You can do it, Charlie!"

"Come on, Moose!"

"Go, Hot Dog, go!"

For a moment I hesitate. This is Hot Dog, who nearly eliminated me only a few days ago. But the cheers are contagious. A minute later we are on our feet, berries forgotten, cheering for the Blue team.

The Blues seem to be gaining. No, now it is the Reds. The boy they call Moose is as big as a mountain. And it seems he cannot be moved. Hot Dog's face turns bright pink. His feet are dug stubbornly in the dirt. But very slowly, the Red team is dragging the Blue team toward the line.

This cannot be. I won't allow it to happen. Not me, Merciless Marvin the Muscular. I dart out and grab the end of rope that trails behind the smallest camper on the Blue team. I plant my paws and pull.

"*Aarggh!*" I give a tremendous heave. But the Reds refuse to budge.

Well, no one said it would be easy. There are about fifteen strong boys on the other end of that rope. Plus one Moose.

"*Ooggh!*" I pull with all my power.

Something is starting to happen. At first it is just the slightest ripple in the rope. Then I take a staggering step backward. And another. I am doing it! Single-handedly, I have turned the tide for the Blue team.

A cheer starts to go up. We must be crossing the line.

Then all at once the rope gives way. Boys topple backward like falling dominoes. With a great thrashing of arms and legs, they collapse in a pile. And there I am at the bottom of the pile, squashed beneath the smallest camper.

"Hooray for Blue!" A mighty cheer fills the air.

I wiggle my way out, struggle to my feet, and bow low.

"Way to go, Charlie!"

"Nice job, Jeremy!"

"That was muscle, Mike and Hot Dog and Randy and Jeff!"

They seem to have forgotten my name.

"Marvin! Have you gone mad?"

It is Raymond, pulling me by the tail into the blackberry bush.

"But I did it! I won the tug-of-war! I was just taking a bow."

Raymond frowns at me over his spectacles. "You know, Marvin, that mice can't afford to take bows."

It is true. This I know from sad experience. It is when you pause to take a bow that the mousetrap snaps shut, the cat pounces, the carving knife goes whistling by your tail. To stay alive, a mouse must be fast of foot and agile of brain and—most of all—invisible to the human eye. This is one of the hard facts of mouse life.

"Sorry," I tell Raymond, "I lost my head."

My gang gives me a small private cheer, and I take a bow. And then we are off to watch the baseball game.

The players are just warming up, tossing a ball around. The Blue pitcher is on the mound, throwing his practice pitches. And crouching behind home plate, wearing his Mets cap and his well-oiled new catcher's mitt, is Sam.

We find seats in the tall grass nearby, so we can cheer him on.

"Play ball!" cries the umpire. And the baseball game is under way.

It turns out to be an exciting one. There are inside-the-park home runs and wild pitches and amazing diving catches. There are headfirst slides into bases and runners thrown out at home plate. And that is only the first inning.

The Red team takes an early lead. But then in the third inning, the Blue team comes storming back. Two innings later, the Red team bounces back on a monstrous home run by the boy they call Moose.

Back and forth goes the lead. Finally, it is the last inning. The Blue team is winning, 17–16. If they can just hang on, they will win the game. But can they hang on? The pitcher is looking tired. Sam is looking dusty. Everyone is looking hot. The first baseman

161

taps his fist into his glove. "Three more outs," he says, "and we can go swimming."

The first Red batter strikes out. Two more to go.

The second batter flies out. One more to go.

The third batter steps up to the plate. Suddenly, from the Red team's cheering section, a chant begins. "Moose! Moose! Moose!"

Moose taps his bat on the plate. In his hands, it looks like a toothpick. He takes a couple of practice swings. Under his T-shirt, huge muscles ripple. This guy looks like a tough out.

The Blue pitcher goes into his windup. He throws.

Moose swings. And he hits a long fly ball to right field. The right fielder runs back. He leaps high in the air. But the ball is over his head.

Moose is around first base, heading for second.

The right fielder is chasing the ball.

Moose rounds second base, just as the right fielder picks up the ball and throws it in. But the throw is wild. The ball bounces in the dirt, caroms off the pitcher's knee, and rolls into the grass behind home plate. Sam is looking for it. Moose is racing around third base.

"Run, Moose, run!"

"Go, Sam!"

Sam still can't find the ball.

"I see it!" Fats suddenly exclaims.

And then I do too—a white baseball hidden in a clump of tall weeds.

The three of us leap up. We get behind that ball.

"One, two, three, heave!" I shout. But this is no Ping-Pong ball. It barely budges. "Again!" I cry. We push with all our might. And finally it starts to roll, out of the weeds, out of the grass, right into Sam's mitt.

Moose slides.

Sam blocks the plate.

They both go down in a swirl of arms and legs.

As the dust clears, the umpire's arm goes up. "Out!" he calls.

The cheers that break out then are the loudest I've heard since BoBo the circus clown paid a visit to Macy's toy department. Campers are jumping up and down, slapping one another on the back. Sam is surrounded by the Blue team, all yelling, "You did it!" "Great game!" "Just outstanding!"

Raymond and Fats and I look at one another. We know who really won the game for the Blue team. But we can't take a bow. Instead, we solemnly shake hands.

"Great game," I tell my gang. "Just outstanding."

14

I Taste Victory Once More

Baseball and basketball and soccer games, Field Day and water sports are over. Now we come to the last big event of Color War—and the best, according to Hot Dog. This is the night of songs and skits and story telling, whistling contests and pie-eating contests. It is the Red and Blue campfire.

Once again we follow in the campers' footsteps on the winding path through the woods. A fat yellow moon sits above the treetops. The air is filled with insect songs. This time we do not tremble and peer over our shoulders at each rustling leaf and snapping twig. The night feels friendly.

There is the clearing and the bright blazing camp-fire. We take our seats on a fallen log at the very edge of the circle of light.

"Let the contests begin!" I proclaim.

The first event is the songwriting contest. Each cabin has written a fight song, which they are to perform. Kevin has been working on his all week. This is his big moment.

> *"Go, Blue!*
> *What a crew!*
> *Stick together just like glue!*
> *If you don't win, I'll sure be blue!"*

This song, as performed by the campers of Red Oak cabin, causes Raymond to shudder and Fats to cover his ears with his paws.

But the next song, sung by Spruce cabin, is even worse.

> *"Fight, fight, fight, fight!*
> *Fight, fight, fight, fight!*
> *Beat Blue!"*

And the next, by Hickory, is pretty awful too.

> *"Red, you should have stayed in bed!"*

By the time fourteen cabins have sung their fight

songs, the three of us are holding our ears and begging for mercy.

"You know," Raymond says, "Kevin might have a chance, after all."

When the winners are announced, Red Oak comes in third.

After that is more music: the whistling contest. Only it turns out that the contestants have to whistle after stuffing their mouths with crackers. Not very many can do it. The sounds that come out are a strange collection of squeaks and bleats and honks. A boy from the youngest cabin, who has the loudest whistle I've ever heard, wins this one.

Then come the skits, put on by the older campers and counselors. Boys are dressed up as bears and as the camp cook and even as garbage cans. Barney the camp dog is dressed up as a mermaid. The woods ring with cheers and laughter. Fats laughs so hard, he rolls off our log.

A few minutes later, everything is quiet as the ghost-story-telling contest begins.

"Once upon a time there was a man who had no head. On his shoulders, instead of a head, he had a carved orange pumpkin. . . ."

It is so still now that you can hear a pine needle drop.

"*. . . Deeper and deeper he went into the forest. Branches tore at his clothing. Vines twined around his legs. And then he heard a sound that sent chills up his spine:* 'Ah-ooooo!' "

Some of the smaller campers are squirming on their benches.

"*. . . He climbed the stairs.* Squee-eeak! *Now he was at the front door. He lifted the latch.* Crrr-eeak! *Inside, everything was black. He struck a match. And there, on the floor of the cabin—*"

"Stop!" cries Fats, twitching and trembling. "I can't take it anymore!" He claps his paws over his ears.

I scowl at him. "Tough guys aren't scared of a little ghost story."

"What? I can't hear you!"

I remove his paws from his ears. "What are you, anyway? A tough guy or a marshmallow?"

"Marshmallows? You say, marshmallows?" Fats perks right up. "Take me to them!"

I give up. And I missed the end of the ghost story too. Now I'll never know what was on the cabin floor.

Finally we come to the contest that we, and Red Oak cabin, have been waiting for: the pie-eating contest. Hot Dog has been starving himself all day for this moment.

The contestants all gather around a long picnic table near the campfire. In the center of the table is a row of pies, a big pile of napkins, and some forks.

"Mmmm!" Fats sniffs the air. "Blueberry!"

"Come on, Hot Dog!" cheer the campers from Red Oak cabin.

"You can do it, Jimmy!" shout some other boys.

The contestants take their places. They pick up their forks.

"Are you ready?" a counselor asks. "On your mark! Set! Pig out!"

He blows his whistle, and immediately each contestant digs into a pie. Forks go flying. Mouths turn rapidly blue.

"Way to go, Hot Dog!"

Hot Dog has already finished his first pie and is reaching for a second. So is the boy named Jimmy. Now forks are forgotten. The contestants are picking up slices of pie and shoving it in with their bare hands.

"Stuff it in, Jimmy!"

Some of the boys are slowing down, but not Jimmy or Hot Dog. They are both starting on their third pie. Their faces are blue. Their T-shirts are blue. Where is all this pie going? Fats looks stunned. Even he has never witnessed such gluttony.

"More! More! More!" chant the campers.

Now all the other contestants have dropped out, looking green under the blue. But Hot Dog and Jimmy are matching each other bite for bite.

Three-and-a-half pies. Four pies.

They each reach for their fifth pie. Hot Dog takes a bite. Jimmy raises a slice to his mouth. But then he stops. He can't do it. He can't eat another bite.

"Hooray for Hot Dog!" cheer the Red Oak campers. And then everyone is cheering.

Hot Dog takes a bow. "I think I need to lie down," he whispers.

This is the last event of Color War. The camp director and the counselors huddle in a circle for a few minutes. And then the camp director steps up next to the campfire. He is holding something in his hands. It is large and gold and seems to have wings.

"It's been a terrific week of Color War," he tells the campers. "We had fabulous swimming and canoe races, great games of basketball, baseball, and soccer. And a lot of fun with Field Day. Now it's time to announce the winning team. The score has been close. The Red and Blue teams have been neck and neck all the way. But this year's trophy goes to—the Blue team!"

The woods echo with yells and cheers, whistles and high fives. And my gang and I are applauding as loudly as the campers. We did it! We brought home the trophy for the Blue team. With a little help from Hot Dog.

They bring on the food then. More pie and lemonade and—"Oh, goody!" cries Fats—marshmallows. The boys start roasting marshmallows and making s'mores, and we celebrate our victory with a glorious feast.

At last the campfire is burning low. Fats has consumed seven s'mores and has been declared the winner of our own personal s'mores-eating contest. "No more ever again!" he moans, collapsing on our log. I stretch out next to him, filled to the brim with blueberry pie and lemonade and marshmallows, not to mention the thrill of victory.

"Gang," I say drowsily.

"Yes, Marvin?" comes Raymond's muffled voice.

And then I say something that astonishes even me. "I like camp."

15

I Head Home at Last

Three days later, as we step out the screen door of the cabin, something red comes fluttering down from the sky.

"A maple leaf," observes Raymond, picking it up. "Just what I need for my leaf collection."

A red maple leaf. What do I know about a red maple leaf? And then my steel trap of a mind remembers. "When the first leaves turn red on the maple trees," Ellsworth said, "the camp closes down."

Is it possible? Can our long summer in the country really be nearing an end?

A breeze rustles through the maple leaves, and all at once I feel a chill in the air.

"Brrrrrr," I shiver.

"Fall is coming," remarks Raymond.

That night, after the campers are in bed, we overhear Sam and Kevin talking.

"Can you believe it? Only four more days of camp."

"Only one more baseball game."

"And one more hike."

"And then we'll be on the bus on our way home to New York City."

So it is true. The day I have longed for is finally at hand. No more dreary peace and quiet. No more wide open empty spaces. No more sniffling and sneezing. No more boring diet of sweets and more sweets. No more wild animals eager to eat us for breakfast.

But no more baseball. No more waterskiing. No more campfires. Strangely, I don't feel quite as excited as I expected.

The next few days are filled with activities done for the last time.

"Our last canoe ride," sighs Raymond, paddling along the shore on a morning without a cloud in the sky or a ripple on the lake.

"Our last care package," laments Fats, one paw in a bag of caramel-covered popcorn, the other in a box of peppermint patties.

"My last chance at waterskiing," I mutter, performing my latest trick, a complete turnaround in midair while jumping over a wave. "I could have been a star."

We attend Sam's final baseball game and play our own last game in the living room. We pick our last blackberries. While we are in the meadow, we drop in to say good-bye to Ellsworth.

"Are you sure you won't stay?" he asks. "Winter is beautiful in Vermont, you know. So quiet and peaceful. Not a human being for miles around. And snow drifting as high as the cabin windows, sometimes as high as the roofs. There is nothing to do but curl up in your cozy hole, munch on delicious dried seeds, and dream the days away."

Dream? This sounds like a nightmare to me. Even more peace and quiet. No people, no action. Nothing but snow and seeds.

Suddenly I can't wait for the bus to New York City.

"Sorry, Ellsworth," I say firmly. "We have to go."

Abigail and the little mice wave good-bye. Ellsworth walks us to the edge of the meadow.

"Good-bye, Marvin and Raymond and Fats! I won't forget you!"

"Good-bye, Ellsworth!"

The last we see of him is the tip of his tail, waving in the tall grass.

And then it is the morning of our very last day of camp. As usual, I am awakened by the rude sounds of reveille. I yawn and stretch, thinking of the day ahead. We will have time for leisurely packing, a swim, maybe a game of catch with our Ping-Pong ball.

I hear Mark's voice, urging the campers out of bed.

"Okay, men. This is the moment you've been waiting for. The Last Clean-up."

This is not possible. They wouldn't do this to us. But a few minutes later, there is the all-too-familiar whisk of brooms, swish of mops, clank of pails. And the campers complaining, "Who are we cleaning this place up for, the chipmunks?"

"Uh-oh, gang," I say. "Here we go again."

So once more we are forced to evacuate. I manage to grab the Ping-Pong ball, Fats a few kernels of popcorn, and Raymond his baseball cards. But we leave everything else behind.

"My collections!" moans Raymond. "My leaves. My bird feathers. My pressed flowers. My fishing lures. My lanyards. My Cracker Jack prizes."

"You could never carry all of that home on the bus," I remind him.

"I was going to pack a trunk," Raymond replies

175

mournfully. "Just like all the campers."

Worst of all, we have to spend another night in the chipmunk hole.

The next morning I awake bright and early, or maybe I never went to sleep. Our few possessions are packed. We are ready to leave.

Bang! The screen door opens. Luggage is tossed outside. Suitcases and trunks, knapsacks and duffel bags and shopping bags. Boys run in and out. And soon there is a pile of luggage like a mountain in front of Red Oak cabin.

Near the top of the mountain, I spot a familiar green knapsack. "There it is!" I hiss. "Let's go, gang!"

Up a scratched black trunk we climb, over a bulging duffel bag. We scale a tan suitcase tied together with rope, another well-stuffed duffel bag, and we've reached the peak. And there is Sam's knapsack. Under the flap we crawl, and drop down inside.

"Ouch!" I land on a sharp pointed object. It's a pinecone. Why would Sam take a dumb pinecone home to New York City?

He is taking home so much stuff, there is barely room for us. His catcher's mitt, of course. His Mets cap. More prickly pinecones, sharp rocks, a pair of scratchy bookends that he made in arts and crafts, three clay pots, an Indian arrowhead, a roll of birch bark, two frogs in a jar, and a bunch of dirty laundry.

Fats wrinkles his nose. "Is it the frogs or the socks that smell so bad?"

It's going to be a long ride home, I can tell.

"Okay, guys," booms Mark's voice. "Let's get these bags down the hill."

Suddenly the mountain of luggage is moving. Our long ride home is under way.

We bounce along for a while, down the hill. Then everything seems to come to a halt. I extract myself from the clutches of Sam's baseball cap and come up for a breath of air. That is when I smell it. It is a smell more pungent than frogs, more powerful than dirty laundry. It is a smell I have yearned for all these weeks: bus fumes.

I can't resist poking my head out to take a look. Yes, there it is. Long and high and bright red, with a black stripe down its side. It has giant wheels and headlights like great staring eyes. And above them, a sign that reads: NEW YORK CITY. Our bus is finally here.

Everyone is standing around near the lodge: campers and counselors, the camp director, Barney the camp dog. They are all saying good-bye.

"Have a good year! See you next summer!"

"Don't forget to write!"

"So long, guys. It was great!"

Fats joins me at the flap. "It *was* great," he says softly. "Delicious, in fact."

"So long, Camp Moose-a-honk," adds Raymond, a tear in his eye.

If there is one thing I can't stand, it is good-byes. "Come on, guys," I grumble. "Let's get this bus on the road."

"Marvin!" Raymond pokes me suddenly in the ribs. "Do you see what I see?"

"What?"

"A baseball card. Someone dropped it. It looks like . . . It might be . . . It's Mike McCloskey!"

"Who is Mike McCloskey?" I ask.

"Only the all-time strikeout king. The winningest pitcher in the major leagues. The best ever in the history of baseball."

I look where Raymond is looking. I see a square of colored cardboard lying under a tree. Mike McCloskey, strikeout king.

I do not hesitate. Without regard for my personal safety, I jump out of the knapsack, slide down a red plaid suitcase, and hit the ground running.

In and out of legs I weave. I dodge a high-top

basketball sneaker, detour around a tennis racket, step over a baseball bat. Then, just as I reach the tree, I come face-to-face with a large black floppy ear, a wet sniffing nose.

"Barney!" I say brightly. "Just the dog I was hoping to see. I wanted to say good-bye. And thanks for all the rides. It was great. Well, so long."

As I am talking, I keep moving. And before he can blink, I've detoured around him too.

There is Mike McCloskey, the strikeout king. I snatch him up, turn, and run.

And then I stop. What happened? Where is everybody?

The bus! While my back was turned, the campers have climbed on board. The driver is in his seat. The engine is running. The counselors are already waving.

They can't do this. They can't leave without me.

I catch sight of something green next to the bus steps. It is Sam's knapsack. I race after it. But it is moving. I cover that ground like I am stealing second base. Now the knapsack is disappearing up the bus steps. I put on a last desperate burst of speed. I leap. I grab. And I catch hold of a dangling strap, just as the bus door slams shut.

I made it.

Raymond and Fats haul me inside.

"Are you all right?" Fats asks.

Raymond shakes his head. "I thought you were going to spend the winter with Ellsworth after all."

"Here," I say. And I present him with Mike McCloskey.

After this, the trip home is a piece of cake. We ride in comfort in the overhead luggage rack. Sprawled out on top of the knapsack, nibbling on popcorn, we listen to the campers singing camp songs and telling camp stories and watch the miles roll by.

For a long time there is nothing to see but trees. Then there are a few houses mixed in. Then there are more and more houses. And stores. And apartment buildings and office buildings and shopping centers.

And then I feel Raymond beside me take a sharp breath.

"Look," he says.

There in the distance, outlined against a deep blue sky, are the towers of a great city. These are not like the apartments and office buildings we saw before. They are so tall, they seem to reach for the clouds. They scrape against the sky. They gleam in the afternoon sun. They beckon to me.

"New York City," I whisper.

An hour later, the bus pulls up under the awning of a hotel in midtown Manhattan. We hitch a last ride in Sam's knapsack, down the bus steps onto the sidewalk. And then he is surrounded by his mother and father and sister, all hugging and exclaiming, "You're here! Let me look at you! Did you have a good time?"

We climb out of the knapsack and are surrounded by New York City.

Horns are honking. Traffic lights are flashing. Taxis are darting here and there. In the distance I hear the familiar wail of a fire engine. People bustle by on the sidewalk, everyone in a hurry, going somewhere. And all around us are tall buildings. Looking up between skyscrapers, I can barely make out a tiny sliver of sky.

I take a deep breath. Mmmm, bus fumes. Hot dogs and sauerkraut. Soot. Corned beef on rye with—yes!—a kosher dill pickle on the side. Police horses. Perfume. Chinese egg rolls. A touch of garbage. And a hundred other intriguing aromas.

We are really home.

Kevin and Sam are saying good-bye. Sam's family is loading his luggage into a taxi. Still talking and laughing, they all climb in.

"Good-bye, Sam!" Raymond and Fats keep on waving until the taxi disappears in traffic.

"Good-bye, Sam," I echo. "Hello, New York!"

Then off we go to the corner to catch the subway to Macy's.